Opening the door quietly, Kate stepped inside. The team was focused on the dark-suited man talking at the head of the table.

His face was in profile, but he turned and stopped speaking as Kate entered, and she was blasted by the full force of his gaze. Pinned in place by topaz eyes. Oh. No. Saturday night's casual encounter was her new boss? Surely it wasn't possible. Perhaps he just *looked* like that guy because he'd invaded her mind.

"Good morning, Ms…?"

His aftershave wafted beneath her nose. Expensive. Spicy. Familiar.

She clenched her hands together and dared to look straight into those eyes she was already too well acquainted with. She schooled her voice to chilly formality as she said, "Kate Fielding."

"Ah. Kate." He nodded, his eyes imprisoning hers for what was probably only a second or two, but it felt agonizingly like minutes. "Damon Gillespie. You were incommunicado yesterday. Was it an eventful Saturday night?"

Even if at times work is rather boring,
there is one person making the office a whole
lot more interesting: the boss!

Dark and dangerous, alpha and powerful,
rich and ruthless… He's in control, he knows
what he wants and he's going to get it!
He's tall, handsome and breathtakingly attractive.
And there's one outcome that's never in doubt—
the heroines of these supersexy
stories will be:

*From sensible suits...into satin sheets!*

Available only from Harlequin Presents®!

# Anne Oliver

## HOT BOSS, WICKED NIGHTS

*Undressed*
BY THE BOSS

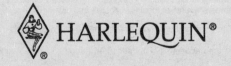

# HARLEQUIN®

TORONTO • NEW YORK • LONDON
AMSTERDAM • PARIS • SYDNEY • HAMBURG
STOCKHOLM • ATHENS • TOKYO • MILAN • MADRID
PRAGUE • WARSAW • BUDAPEST • AUCKLAND

Recycling programs
for this product may
not exist in your area.

ISBN-13: 978-0-373-12865-5

HOT BOSS, WICKED NIGHTS

First North American Publication 2009.

Copyright © 2009 by Anne Oliver.

www.eHarlequin.com

Printed in U.S.A.

**All about the author...**
*Anne Oliver*

When not teaching or writing, **ANNE OLIVER**
loves nothing more than escaping into
a book. She keeps a box of tissues handy—
her favorite stories are intense, passionate,
against-all-odds romances. Eight years ago
she began creating her own characters in
paranormal and time-travel adventures, before
turning to contemporary romance. Other
interests include quilting, astronomy, all things
Scottish and eating anything she doesn't have
to cook. Sharing her characters' journeys with
readers all over the world is a privilege...and a
dream come true. Anne lives in Adelaide, South
Australia, and has two adult children. Visit her
Web site at www.anne-oliver.com. She loves
to hear from readers. E-mail her at
anne@anne-oliver.com.

Many thanks to Meg Sleightholme
for her invaluable assistance.

# CHAPTER ONE

A *CONDOM*? Kate stared into the organza pouch that the inebriated vestal virgin—aka the bride-to-be—had just dangled on her finger as if it were about to spontaneously combust.

She ignored the other recipients' smirks—all single girlfriends who appreciated the humour—but her free hand fisted with embarrassment against the filmy skirt of her belly-dancer's costume. Hen dos and their sexual innuendoes weren't her thing. How was straight-down-the-line all-work-and-no-play Kate Fielding going to cope with the rest of the evening with a condom burning a hole in her hand? Even if it was disguised as a lavender bag.

Thank goodness most of her face was veiled because she could feel a riot of crimson exploding into her cheeks. 'Ah…I um…'

'Go for it, Kate,' Sheri-Lee told her. 'You only live once.' While Kate stood speechless, Sheri snatched the tiny organza pouch from Kate's fingers and tucked it out of sight beneath the beaded waistband of her friend's skirt against her right hip. 'Casually single until you meet Mr Right.'

A chorus of girly giggles broke out as if the idea was absurd. Kate couldn't help feeling a little hurt. And self-conscious. Was she the only one here over twenty-one?

'Thanks…I think.' A strangled laugh escaped her and she looked longingly towards the door. She noticed some of the girls had spilled out of the private room in search of male company and were mingling with hotel patrons near the bar. *Escape.* Before anyone else could elaborate on the sad status of her life. 'Excuse me, I just need…' *A breather.* Her costume jingled as she ducked around an Amazon warrior queen and Cleopatra, then squeezed past what looked like a female version of a sixties Russian spy.

She let out a sigh as cooler air enveloped her. Less raucous here. Dim lighting lent an intimate atmosphere to the quaint but tiny turn-of-the-century pub in Sydney's trendy suburb of Paddington, a few steps from Kate's office. Wandering to the wall plastered with its familiar framed pictures of the pub in its early years, she sipped the champagne she'd been holding for over an hour. But she wasn't seeing them, she was seeing her ex-fiancé.

Every hen night evoked the same sharp reminders. She should be married with kids by now. Her sister—her much *younger* sister, Rosa—was going to beat her to it. No thanks to Nick.

She shook her head. She was *not* going to think about Nick. Or how he'd betrayed her with another woman after she'd given him three years of her life. Three *precious* child-bearing years. And she was *happy* Rosa had found true love.

So what if Kate had turned thirty last month and—if her father's attitude was anything to go by—was rushing headlong into spinsterhood? Since Nick's defection Kate had never deviated from the narrow path she'd set herself and walked on the wild side. Her choice, she reminded herself, and a *good* thing. But the little bump of the organza bag against her hip stirred something hot and primal deep in her belly, calling up other times…

*Oh…drat.*

The aromas of Italian and Middle Eastern cuisine mingled on the air as suppertime approached. She wished it would hurry up so she could make her excuses and leave.

Sheri-Lee had met her Mr Right. She was getting married

and leaving work and she was doing both next week. Still, Kate wondered…Why did marriage often mean the end of paid employment? Independence?

She almost felt sorry for Sheri-Lee. Love always seemed to involve sacrifice, *women's* sacrifice. Except that Sheri radiated happiness and couldn't wait to resign and set up house.

Four years ago Kate had nearly fallen into that trap herself. Forget that she'd have fallen willingly, safe in the knowledge that Nick loved her. In hindsight she knew it hadn't been love at all on his part.

So…casually single?

*Dream on, Kate.* She didn't have time for men. Nor had she ever entirely understood the attraction of casual sex, but, honestly, sometimes her ego needed a little stroking…

A tingle danced down her spine, hot and cold at the same time, like a hot fudge sundae, touching every vertebra in turn with the shivery sensation. Someone was watching her; she could feel it. And it felt like one hundred per cent pure masculine interest.

She resisted an involuntary shudder as she cast her eyes over her shoulder.

Then she saw him, and understanding dawned bright and hot. The six-foot-something dream in jungle-green army-surplus pants, black T-shirt and scuffed boots looking at her. Tanned and unshaven with dark hair. Topaz eyes.

The reason for the tingle.

And the reason her heart was knocking against her ribs. The suddenly damp palms. He was the reason for a whole lot of deliciously wicked things happening to her body right now. Oh, yeah, she could do casual and her ego wouldn't mind one bit if *he* was the one doing the stroking.

She turned slowly, her champagne flute all but forgotten in her hands as she eyed him back from behind the safety of her disguise. Did this guy work out or what? His T-shirt clung like a lover to his well-sculpted body, the sleeves stretched tight over hard muscle and olive skin. He looked as if he'd just stepped out of an adventure movie.

A glance lower suggested his legs were in as good a shape as the rest of him, but the baggy trousers kept the details a mystery. She looked up in time to see his gaze centred near her exposed navel. His frank appraisal as his eyes drifted to the gauzy folds of her skirt and the outline of her legs seared her skin with liquid heat, sending bubbles of lava-lust through her veins and leaving her gasping for air in the suddenly overheated room.

She'd never felt this reaction to a man's attention before. Weak. Wanton. Willing. She was totally out of her depth. Not only did he look dangerous, she had no doubt he was because any moment now she'd melt at the base of those size twenty-something work-scuffed boots.

And those boots were making their way towards her.

She straightened to her full five feet four inches. Obviously he wasn't into style, since he hadn't bothered to conform to anything remotely resembling the expected neat casual dress code. Still, she was prepared to overlook that one small infraction since he more than made up for it in other ways.

*Go for it.* Sheri's words chimed in her head. *Casually single until you meet Mr Right.*

By the time he'd reached her, she had her nerves under control. Almost. Until she found herself looking up—way up—into those eyes. At this distance she could see flecks of green in his gold irises and lines feathering from the corners that spoke of time in the outdoors or fatigue, or both. He smelled of sweat and heat and testosterone.

'Can I get you something?' he said, in a deep sexy rumble that matched the rest of him.

Something? Like excited? Her neglected libido sighed. He could get her anything he pleased. Anywhere, any time.

'A drink,' he clarified, nodding at her half-empty glass when she didn't reply. 'Looks like you could do with a refill.'

Uh oh, he was chatting her up and this was *real life*, not a daydream. Her bravado dipped, her fingers tightened on the glass. 'Ah…I'm fine for the moment. Thank you.'

From the corner of her eye she saw a couple of the girls watching with interest. Waiting to see if she'd bolt, no doubt. So she forced herself to remain still.

His gaze dropped to her mouth—or where her mouth would be—and his brows lowered fractionally. She could see him pondering the etiquette of lifting her veil, and deflected his thoughts with a quick, 'You look as if you've just flown halfway around the world.'

Her accusatory tone triggered a full-wattage smile from him, which in turn triggered another hike in her pulse rate.

'In fact I'm just in from LA.' The sinews in his forearm twisted as he checked his watch. 'As of two hours ago.'

Okay, so that was the reason for the unkempt look. 'Work or pleasure?'

'Both.' He cocked his head. 'I assume you're with the fancy-dress party-goers?'

She shrugged and smiled back. 'A hen night.'

He leaned forward slightly so that his head was closer to hers. 'Not yours, I hope.'

'No.' Her heart pounded once, hard. Through the gauze she could smell a hint of residual aftershave now—something spicy and expensive—at odds with his rugged appearance.

'That's the best news I've heard all day,' he said, and one hard, callused hand wrapped around Kate's—the one clutching her champagne flute. Electricity arced between their fingers, sending sparks shooting up her arm. Her eyes jerked to his and locked into his magnetic gaze. She felt the power in his fingers as he raised the glass. Felt his warm breath on her hand as he held the crystal tantalisingly close to his mouth. A slight movement on her part and she'd feel the scrape of his dark stubble against her skin.

Somewhere over her shoulder she heard a squeak of suppressed mirth. Her friends thought this was amusing? Well, she'd show them. She'd make something of tonight, with the man about to share her drink. This might be her last chance. A chance to show everyone, including herself, that she wasn't over the hill yet.

And…if she hid Kate Fielding tonight, she could partake of some of that casual fun she'd been missing out on. Have her ego stroked. *Ooh, yes.* For a little while she could be whoever she wanted with him.

*For* him.

Damon Gillespie was suddenly very glad he'd arrived in Sydney three days early. He'd been about to have a drink at the bar, take a quick look at the premises he'd come to Sydney to see, then hit the sack before tackling the business side tomorrow, but he'd walked into a costume party.

And seen her.

She'd looked… Not lonely, but alone. Definitely alone. Like him. Maybe that was the reason she aroused more than simple lust in him. But what?

Shrugging off the oddly disquieting feeling, he pressed their joined fingers against the stem of the glass. Forgot about jet lag and sleep deprivation and concentrated on the purely physical. The sensation of her knuckles locked like grim death beneath his, the subtle Oriental scent wafting from her costume as his gaze roamed over her once more.

Business could wait.

With most of her face covered, he had only a misty temptation to go by. Glimpses of a straight nose and high cheekbones, generous lips.

Ample female flesh spilled out of her bra top, bells and beads twinkling beneath the lights even as she drew breath. Her skirt—twenty or so gauzy scarfs in saffron and gold—sat low on her hips, showcasing her tiny waist and a glorious expanse of flat belly and golden skin, not to mention the outline of a perfect pair of legs. What intrigued him most was the ruby stone where her navel should be. How the deuce did she keep it there? he wondered. Some pelvic muscular trick?

His body tightened and the familiar rush of adrenaline he experienced before a jump rushed through his veins. Back in Oz two hours and he'd found a living fantasy. It had been a long time. He'd been too busy expanding his latest project and chasing his hunger for extreme sports across the globe to indulge in female company.

He intended to rectify that. Tonight.

He lifted the glass—and her fingers—to his lips and searched her eyes for a response. Framed with heavy mascara and navy eyeliner, they looked huge, and an honest-to-goodness lust flickered in their midnight depths. Spanish eyes, he thought, and from the recesses of his memory flashed another pair of dark eyes. He willed it away, pressed his lips to the flute and swallowed.

He could taste her on the glass. Sweet with a hint of tart. But the champagne… He grimaced in distaste. 'Champagne should be chilled.' He pried her fingers from the glass, set it on a passing drinks waiter's tray and swapped it for a fresh one. 'Here you go.'

The tips of her fingers brushed his as he handed it to her. 'Thank you.'

He reached for her free hand. 'Come on, Little Egypt, let's find somewhere quieter.' He led her around the bar, past the crowd to a corner of the room near a large potted philodendron where the noise was less intrusive. He waited for her to pull her veil aside and take that first sip. But she lifted the glass *inside* the gauze and her face remained that tempting mystery.

He hissed out an almost silent breath of frustration through his teeth. 'What's your name?'

She sipped a moment, then said, 'Shakira.'

The way she said it, smoky and seductive, added fuel to a fire that wasn't going to be extinguished without some serious action.

'Okay, *Shakira…*' Taking a step closer, he slid his hand beneath her disguise and caught her chin between thumb and forefinger. Tilted her head so he could see what he could of her properly. He heard her little catch of breath and a smooth hand wrapped around his forearm.

'*No.*'

Her dark eyes flashed, but he soothed her with a smile and shook his head. 'It's okay. We can play it your way.' *So long as we can play.* She relaxed her hold and let his thumb trace the plump fullness of her lower lip. Once, twice. He paused as a thought occurred to him. 'Unless the reason's a jealous boyfriend somewhere that you're cheating on?'

He felt her jaw stiffen beneath his fingers. As if she'd been burned before, he thought.

'I don't cheat.'

'Good.' He couldn't begin to say how much that pleased him. 'Neither do I.'

He manoeuvred her so that the foliage shielded them from the majority of party-goers, then leaned in to absorb more of that exotic perfume. Frangipani and summer. It wound through his senses like one of those chiffon scarves covering her legs.

How could such an alluring woman be unattached? *Don't ask questions, just enjoy the ride.* He nuzzled her neck, then, encouraged by her response, nipped the fragrant flesh beneath her ear. The little bells on her costume tinkled against the front of his trousers, her beaded bra abraded his chest, her feminine curves felt soft and sensual against his hardening body.

He slid a finger just above the band of her skirt from one pelvic bone to the other over firm, flat belly. Her flesh rippled and quivered beneath his touch, sending molten heat fizzing to his groin.

Her eyes flared with the same hot need that surged through him. He was so turned on, if he wasn't careful, he'd come right here in front of her, not to mention a roomful of people. He wanted that belly against his. Naked. He wanted her rippling and quivering around him as he pumped into her. And he wanted it now.

With difficulty he stepped back. He knew by her eyes and her elevated breathing that she too resented the loss of contact. That she was as eager—and willing—as he. He grabbed her hand. 'Let's get out of here.'

Kate heard a collective gasp somewhere behind her but she felt too weak, too unbalanced, to do anything but allow him to tug her along the hallway beyond the bar. They passed a waitress bearing a tray of tempting hors d'oeuvres, the spicy aroma wafting behind her.

She struggled to keep up with his long strides in her wedge-heeled sandals. Up a narrow flight of stairs. The knowledge of what she was about to do pumped through her veins. She'd never been so physically attracted to anyone on sight before and, yes, Sheri, you only lived once.

He stopped at the second door they came to, produced a key from his pocket. The instant he opened the door, he whirled her inside, plunging them into almost total darkness. She heard the lock click behind him. 'Now where were we?' he murmured.

Her eyes adjusted so that she could just make out the broad outline of his shoulders. 'Right about here.' She set her hands on his chest. Correction: *Shakira* set her hands on his chest because Kate Fielding would never do anything so audacious—rubbing her thumbs over the jersey and loving the hot, rock-solid masculine feel of him, leaning in to inhale his scent. She hadn't been this up close to a man's body in a long time.

Light from the street cast a faint silvery glow to the room as he reached for her veil. But it was still dark enough to maintain the integrity of her disguise as he unhooked the loop above her ear and pushed the fabric aside.

He was silent a moment as he traced the shape of her face, her nose, her eyebrows. Her lips. 'You're gorgeous,' he said, and pulled her hard up against his body, trapping her hands. 'Even in the dark, you're one irresistible woman.'

The awe in the softly spoken words thrilled her, excited her. She could feel the hard ridge of masculine flesh against her belly, his heart pounding against her fingertips, her own heart thundering in her ears.

Strong hands gripped her upper arms as his mouth descended on hers. She heard a long low moan—hers?—then an answering rumble that vibrated against her palms. His lips were dry and firm and very, very skilled.

With no persuasion at all, her lips opened beneath his. His tongue invaded her mouth, plunging inside then withdrawing like a promise of anticipated delights. He tasted good. Coffee and peppermint and something richer, darker. Hotter. When he raised his head, she pulled it down again. She wasn't nearly ready to let him go.

But he wasn't going anywhere. His hands moved from her arms to her bare midriff, to her bra—and ended up with a palm-full of brass and tinkles. He inhaled a hiss of impatience and if she hadn't been so breathless she might have laughed at the sheer incredulity of the whole situation.

Nothing was going to stop him. His fingers curled over the tops of her breasts and swept beneath, then down to find her nipples taut and strained against the fabric. He rolled them between his fingers, sending hot darts of need shooting through her body.

She moaned as an echoing tightness swept to her core and leaned forward to give him easier access, which he took with swift efficiency. Her breasts spilled out into his hands. She gazed down, stunned at the sight of his dark hands on her pale flesh.

She looked up at him, glimpsed the firestorm in his eyes before his lips again fused with hers and he was walking her backwards, their legs knocking and tangling until she hit the wall with a jolt. A hard masculine body bumped against hers.

*'Oh-h-h.'*

The pressure eased a little and he lifted his head. 'You okay?'

'Yes-s-s.' Was that hiss of desire hers?

She groaned deep in her throat—with relief, with impatience—as he pressed against her once more, grinding his hips with hers, the ridge of his arousal huge and hot and heavy against her belly.

His hands were at her waist, lifting her as if she weighed nothing, pinning her against the wall and holding her there. Her shoes slipped from her feet with a quiet 'plop' of surrender.

'Wrap your legs around me.'

His hand swept aside the flimsy points of her skirt, the thin strip of fabric covering her centre, the heat and slight roughness of his fingers searing her moist flesh as he claimed her.

She heard the sharp rasp of his zip as he freed himself, the hard, slippery feel of masculinity against the apex of her thighs. He paused, his jaw tightly bunched, eyes fused with hers, his breath a hot rasp against her cheek. 'You're sure?'

She felt imprisoned, helpless, trapped.

She'd never felt more alive, more free, more ready to take that chance. 'Yes.'

'Wait— Protection…' He reached into his pocket.

'Ah…' Her fumbling fingers located the tiny organza bag tucked into her waistband. 'I happen to have…' She pulled out the packet and held it aloft with a grin of triumph.

'Ingenious,' he murmured, regarding her intently as if wondering how many more she had stashed there before taking it from her and quickly sheathing himself.

The thought flickered through her mind to tell him she didn't usually have a ready supply, but she figured a girl of the world like Shakira might. She didn't need to explain herself to him—this was literally a one-night stand. Except that her feet weren't touching the floor at all and her toes were curling up in anticipation.

He guided himself inside her. He was big—*huge*—and she felt tight, stretched, invaded, but she pushed down on him with a gasp of satisfaction.

He thrust up once, twice, with a power and intensity that left her breathless. She clung to his shoulders, her fingers digging into the soft fabric of his T-shirt, the little ornaments on her costume tinkling. Her beaded bra strap felt rough against her back as the rhythmic movements increased.

She was blind and deaf to everything but him. His eyes, the outline of his body in the dimness. The harshness of his breaths as he pushed inside her, the sound of flesh against flesh.

She came just as she felt him shudder his own climax deep inside her. *Oh, good Lord.*

He continued to hold her until their breathing slowed, then she unwound her legs and he lowered her until her feet touched the floor. Her legs were wobbly, her whole body lethargic and limp.

He palmed one still-exposed breast. 'Where do you—?' The buzz of his mobile jarred, cutting him off mid-sentence. 'I have to take this call,' he murmured reluctantly, pulling his phone from the deep recesses of his trouser pockets. He lifted it to his ear with one hand while he continued to stroke one breast back and forth with the other. 'Yes?'

As she watched his eyes turned remote, the outline of his jaw turned to stone. 'Where the hell is it, then?' Abruptly he pulled his hand away, those remote eyes turning hot just for a second as they met hers. 'Stay right here, I'll be back.' Then he crossed the room without a backward glance and opened the door to the bathroom. 'Okay, contact Dark Vertigo.' Pause. 'Forget it, I'll do it myself…' The light came on and Kate blinked against the glare before he closed the door behind him.

In the space of a heartbeat everything changed. Sanity charged back with a vengeance. Leaning against the wall for support, she refastened her veil before he returned and decided to switch on the light, then slid down the cool surface to the floor inch by excruciating inch. She located her sandals and slipped them on. Listened to her pulse beating in her ears, felt its fury in her throat, her nipples, between her thighs.

What had just happened?

*Casual* was what had happened. And thinking about it *now* was just a tad late. What in heaven's name had she done? With a man she'd met less than twenty minutes earlier?

She didn't even know his name.

She closed her eyes. Self-preservation and common sense seemed to have deserted her along with the man. A man she'd never see again, she told herself. *So blame Shakira, put it safely to one side to think about later.*

Right this minute she had to get out. Go home. Now.

Moments later she slipped out to the concierge desk, collected her bag and made a swift exit into the crisp night air.

She texted Sheri-Lee, apologising that she'd had to leave— something unexpected had come up—as she hurried to her car. She'd never done anything so crazy, so irresponsible in her whole thirty years. The breeze chilled any residual heat from her body. She'd always been in an ongoing relationship with a man before they'd made love. A relationship based on mutual respect, honesty and friendship.

And yet one look from that guy had changed her into someone she didn't know. A strange sensation wrapped around her and she rubbed the goose-bumps that sprang up on her arms. It was as if she'd given him not only her body but her soul.

# CHAPTER TWO

DAMON swore silently when he discovered his bedroom empty and the most enchanting creature he'd ever made out with gone. Getting laid on his first night back hadn't been his intention—he wasn't normally a man for one-nighters but one look at her and his brain had taken a swift dive below his belt. He'd had to have her.

He could go back downstairs and see if she was still around, which he doubted. Besides, he never put women before business and he wasn't going to start now. Presumably that was all she'd wanted or she'd have stuck around for an encore. Pity, but—he shrugged—it wasn't as if anything could come of it.

He pulled a beer from the room's bar fridge and popped the top. Walked to the window and looked down at the business he'd crossed the Pacific to deal with. The travel agency his uncle had left him with its less-than-stellar façade and outdated posters. He shook his head. It was precisely why he'd arrived earlier than scheduled—to get a look at the place ahead of time.

Instead, he'd looked straight into a pair of soulful dark eyes and been sucked right under…

*Bonita.* Her image bloomed in his mind, with her father's Spanish eyes and her Egyptian mother's beauty. Was it any wonder he'd been attracted to those same attributes tonight? He took a swig from the bottle but the liquid tasted acrid on his tongue. He'd watched the woman he'd loved die at twenty-four.

And he'd learned the only way to deal with loss was to cut those people close to him out of his heart. Slapping a decisive palm on the window sill, he set the beer down and headed to the bathroom for a long-overdue shower. To ease travel-cramped muscles and wash away the woman's lingering scent. No regrets but no reminders. He was in Sydney to put things right for his uncle, the last act he could perform for what he could call family. Then he was gone.

Thanks to a doozy of a cold, which had hit in the early hours of Sunday morning, Kate was running late for work on Monday—not good when Bryce's nephew was arriving from heaven knew where tomorrow to look over the business. And the traffic this morning was a nightmare.

While she could have been at the office ahead of time making sure the man had nothing to find fault with she'd wasted her entire Sunday sleeping. Or trying to. Even with her mobile switched off and the landline off the hook, the memory of another man had kept her from getting the shut-eye she needed.

*Kate Fielding had had a one-night stand.*

A hot and steamy and *abbreviated* one-night stand. The very idea sent shock waves rocketing through her body. She braked with a squeal of tyres for yet another red light she'd barely noticed. The driver behind leaned on his horn.

Hell. She wiped her nose, gripped the wheel harder. Adventure man wasn't good for her health. Thinking about him wasn't good for her health. What did it matter that he'd put whatever business he was involved in before her? That he was probably like Nick and took his opportunities where he could? She was never going to see him again. She'd enjoyed herself and that was where it ended. That was what casually single was all about, right?

If she could just convince her still-sensitised body of that.

By sheer will she forced the images from her mind. Time to concentrate on the more immediate problem. Tomorrow morning she was going to come face to face with a man she already disliked by reputation and she wasn't going to give him any reason to find fault with her work.

Her boss's sudden death three weeks ago at a young forty-three meant the travel agency faced an uncertain future. She'd worked seven long hard years for the manager's position. Now she had to prove herself again, to some guy whom she'd never met, who more likely than not knew nothing about the travel industry. Certainly he knew nothing about Aussie Essential.

She pulled into her reserved parking space a little too quickly, noting the time on her dashboard as she switched off the ignition. Damn. She grabbed her bag, wiping her nose again as she hurried across the car park in the brisk autumn breeze. Only ten minutes late.

She was never late. Lateness was unprofessional and showed a complete disregard for other people. Her low-heeled shoes echoed impatiently on the concrete. Checking her appearance in the glass door as she entered, she tugged the hem of her navy jacket, adjusted her collar unnecessarily. Smoothed her long hair clasped in a knot at the back of her head out of habit.

'Hi, Deb.' She smiled at their newest team member sitting behind her desk. The *only* team member behind her desk, she noticed. 'Where the heck is everyone?'

'Hi, Kate…umm…' Her eyes flicked to the large office they used as a staffroom behind them.

As Kate stowed her handbag beneath her desk a feeling of doom descended on her. 'Don't tell me. He's here already.'

'He said he tried contacting you…'

'Oh, no…' she groaned. 'I slept through yesterday and I was running so late this morning I didn't stop to check my messages.' Kate's blocked sinuses chose that moment to prickle. She barely caught the explosion with a tissue. Even the cold capsules she'd taken earlier hadn't diffused the throbbing headache and her legs felt like lead. She mopped her nose. 'He wasn't due till tomorrow.'

'I know.' Deb shrugged. 'He called everyone in for an early staff meeting. They're all in there right now. I'm manning the desk—'

Kate tossed her tissue in the bin and grabbed another handful from her desk. 'Excuse me? He called a *staff meeting*?'

*He* being the nephew Bryce only ever mentioned on a couple of occasions that Kate could recall. The globe-trotting adventurer, the man who'd not bothered to come to the funeral but was here now to seize his inheritance.

Deb nodded. 'He seems to have everything under control.'

He had no right to have everything under control. Kate always managed Aussie Essential Travel in Bryce's absence and he'd promised her full authority from next month. That was probably a moot point now. Still, she'd been managing just fine for the past three weeks. What would his nephew, who as far as she knew had never set foot inside this place, know about the travel business?

'Are you okay, Kate?'

Kate shook her head, and winced. But she forced a smile. 'I'm breathing…sort of…I'd better get in there.'

*Calm down,* she ordered herself. *Be professional but assertive. Leave him in no doubt that you're quite capable, thank you very much.* She grabbed a notepad and pen from her desk.

Opening the door quietly, she stepped inside. The team was focused on the dark-suited man talking at the head of the table. His voice was deep and melodic. And authoritative.

She tensed, ready to defend her own authority.

His face was in profile, but he turned and stopped speaking as Kate entered and she was blasted by the full force of his gaze. Pinned in place by topaz eyes. His jaw might have tensed momentarily—or maybe not—she was too busy picking her own jaw off the floor.

Oh. *No*. Her Saturday night's casual encounter was Bryce's nephew? The man she detested by reputation? She felt a sudden tightness in her chest that had nothing to do with her cold. Surely it wasn't possible.

Or Damon Gillespie just *looked* like that guy because he'd invaded her mind. The clean-shaven man in the suit that fitted his broad shoulders to perfection and looked as if it had cost a million bucks and the sombre silk tie *couldn't* be that rugged jungle hero who'd kissed her senseless, made love to her against the wall… She felt that same heat rise up her neck now as the rest of her staff turned to look at her.

*Hold it together.* She took a deep steadying breath and nodded a silent greeting to them. Forget authority, forget assertive—all she wanted to do was slide into the nearest chair with as little fuss as possible and get herself under some sort of control.

On noodle legs, she moved towards the only available chair which, by some unfortunate coincidence, happened to be next to Damon Gillespie's right hand. It was okay, she told herself; he wouldn't recognise her.

To make it worse, he was waiting for her to sit before continuing with whatever it was he was saying, making her the centre of attention. 'I'm interrupting, I'm sorry…' she half whispered and immediately cursed herself for apologising to this man who represented everything she despised. *He* should be the one apologising.

'Good morning, Miz…?'

She reached her destination and sank down, her notepad and pen sliding from her trembling fingers onto the table. His aftershave wafted beneath her nose. Expensive, spicy.

Familiar.

She clenched her hands together and dared to look straight into those eyes she was already too well acquainted with. She schooled her voice to chilly formality as she said, 'Kate Fielding.'

'Ah. Kate.' He nodded, his eyes imprisoning hers for probably only a second or two but it felt agonisingly like minutes. 'Damon Gillespie. You were incommunicado yesterday. An eventful Saturday night?' His tone *almost* suggested he knew all about her Saturday night. Or was it just her perception?

Thank goodness he didn't appear to expect an answer and moved right along in the same breath, informing them that he wanted to meet with each member of staff individually over the next couple of days. Kate noted the details on her pad, more for something to occupy her hands than anything else. But because her hands were shaking, she gave up and clenched them together on her lap.

Damon Gillespie tugged at his snowy white cuffs and spread his hands on the table. Large blunt, short-nailed fingers. Kate tried to look away but she couldn't take her eyes off them. The memory taunted her. Those talented fingers exploring, finding all her pleasure points…

Her pulse throbbed slow and heavy and she bit down on her lower lip. Why was her body betraying her? It had no business feeling all molten and fluid in the middle of a staff meeting. Worse, it was responding to a man she didn't want to like—*didn't* like; loathed, in fact.

She jerked to attention at the mention of her name, knocking her pen to the floor with a resounding clatter in the silent room, and realised he was watching her expectantly, waiting for an answer. 'Ah…I missed that.'

Damon knew she had. Good God, what were the odds of your one-night stand turning up at a staff meeting? She'd been a mess of nerves since she'd realised who he was and if he wasn't mistaken the temperature in the room had dropped a few degrees.

Not the way she'd behaved the last time he'd seen her, he

remembered. No, sir, she'd been more than willing and abundantly able. And hot. She couldn't be sure *he* knew, however, because perhaps she thought she'd disguised herself adequately. She'd obviously not considered the tiny mole below the corner of her left eye. Or the fact that the veil was more transparent than she thought.

He retrieved the pen from the floor, noting the sexy ankles in her unflattering granny shoes as he did so, and set it on her pad. Her dark eyes collided with his as she mumbled a thank-you. 'I asked if there's anyone I need to thank personally for helping out with the funeral arrangements, flowers and donations and such. As you'd know now, Bryce and I had no other relatives.'

'I was aware of that…' Her gaze filled with what looked like pity and held his for a beat out of time. *No need for tea and sympathy,* he assured her silently with an equally resolute gaze.

Then her eyes cooled and skidded away as if she regretted the momentary lapse and she straightened, jotted something else on her notepad, her fingers wrapped so tightly around her pen he wondered that it didn't break. Her voice took on that chilly note again as she said, 'I have the details at home. And the book of attendees.'

There was an emphasis on that last word as if condemning him for not turning up to the funeral. He didn't bother telling her the news of Bryce's death hadn't reached him until a few days ago. 'Thanks, Kate. I'll give you a call later.' He sent a smile her way but she wasn't giving him eye contact.

He turned, swept his gaze over the table as he smiled at each individual in turn and said, 'Thank you, everyone. I think that's it for now. As for Aussie Essential Travel, don't worry. We'll all muddle through this together.'

Hushed conversation ensued as staff members skirted the table. Kate pushed up too, but he laid a restraining hand over one of hers. 'A moment of your time, Kate.' He didn't remove his hand right away, enjoying the feel of her smooth fingers beneath his, even if they were clenched like grim death.

She resented him being here. No, he decided, it was more than that.

He leaned back in his chair and watched her as the room emptied. She stared back at him with unsmiling eyes, a contrast to the dark desire he'd seen there thirty-six hours ago. This conservative Kate with her raven-black hair imprisoned in a tight knot, those gorgeous breasts crammed into a demure navy suit, was no Oriental temptress. Even the no-frills name 'Kate' conjured an entirely different image from the sultry 'Sha-ki-ra'. A double personality.

Maybe a double life? he mused, watching her struggle with a riot of emotions. 'You and Bryce were friends, I'm told.'

'Yes.' She looked down at her hand beneath his, then yanked it away to clench it over her other one on her lap. Her head jerked up, and her eyes flashed, sunlight glinting on ice. 'He was a caring and generous boss. And a true gentleman.'

Ah, well, that last attribute left him out in the cold. As far as she was concerned at any rate, if her expression was anything to go by. Yep, he'd been anything but a gentleman on Saturday night.

And she'd enjoyed every wild and wicked moment, this prim and proper woman in front of him. He felt his mouth kick up at the corner despite himself.

'What are you smiling about?' Before he could draw breath she continued, jamming each word onto a skewer. 'Let me guess. You've just had a business fall into your lap.'

She was, he thought, his half-grin still in place, magnificent in anger.

She was also way off base. He didn't need a failing business; he had enough problems with his own at this moment.

'He's been gone a matter of weeks.' Her voice dropped to a hoarse whisper. 'Have you no respect?'

His facial muscles tightened. If this was about Bry, she wouldn't understand that Damon refused to look back. It didn't mean he didn't mourn Bry's death in his own way. Nor did he have to justify himself to her. 'It's not about respect. Life goes on, Kate.'

She blinked, then sneezed. Snatched the box of tissues on the table. 'Obviously he meant little to you,' she said, swiping at her nose.

'We lived in the same house when I was growing up. He was only nine years older than me; I knew him as well as you'd know a brother.'

'And how long ago was that?'

*Years.* 'I'm living in the US at present, but we kept in contact via email, by phone.' Usually when Bryce wanted extra funds.

She must have had it rough over the past couple of weeks, he thought. Besides, she looked damn unwell. 'You're sick. Go home and take the rest of the day off,' he suggested quietly. 'I'll be in touch later.'

She raised her mascara-stained red eyes and stared at him as if he'd grown horns. 'Who are you to tell me I can take the day off? I haven't had a day off in three years. I'm the most senior staff member here; I can't run away from my responsibilities. People might need me.'

He nodded. He had to admire her dedication. Most employees would be running for their duvets. 'Okay. But if you change your mind, no one'll think badly of you.'

She pushed up, taking the tissue box and notepad with her. 'But *I* would.'

'Hey,' he said softly. 'Go easy on yourself. I'm staying at Bryce's apartment if you need to get in touch.' He took the pad from her hand, scrawled his mobile number beneath her notes.

'I'm sure that won't be necessary,' she replied frostily. 'I can handle any situation should it arise.'

He met her gaze. 'I don't doubt it. But just in case.'

He watched her go, then spent a few moments checking

his messages, made a couple of calls, then slipped out the back way. He unlocked the luxury BMW he'd leased yesterday for the time he'd be here, and sat for a few moments, barely seeing the charming row of Paddington's little terraced houses as Kylie Minogue sang on the stereo.

'What have you got me into, Bry?' he said, staring at the darkening clouds. He'd already injected a six-figure lump sum into Bry's business account a couple of years back. A loan, Bry had said. Where the hell had that money gone?

After collecting the keys from Security at Bryce's apartment yesterday he'd driven to the office and taken a quick look at the figures. Then wished to blazes he hadn't. A decision to shut up shop meant six employees would be out of a job, a situation that didn't sit well with him. After all, turning struggling businesses around was his forte.

The million-dollar question was did he want to spend the time and energy, not to mention yet more of his own capital that the agency would need, here? In Sydney?

He'd grown up here. Lived with his grandmother through most of his adolescence. He'd been a mistake, he'd been told at age five, and he'd never been allowed to forget it. Until Grandma had put her steel-capped foot down and insisted he grow up in a stable environment with her and his father's younger brother while his parents chased storms around the US.

Eventually they'd stopped coming home altogether. The last time he'd seen them was at his grandmother's funeral ten years ago. He had no idea where they were now and he cared even less.

That was what he reminded himself as a chill seemed to wrap around his bones despite the car's warmth. 'I'd have come back sooner, Bry, if I'd known.'

But they'd never been close. Damon had his own life. If it wasn't his Internet business it was deciding where his next thrill-seeking BASE jump would take him. Parachuting off buildings, bridges and mountains—the ultimate extreme sport and the only way to live.

So now he'd inherited a business he didn't want but felt a familial obligation to put right. And an unwanted attraction for a woman who couldn't stand the sight of him.

Yet she'd been all over him like a red-hot rash on Saturday night. Hadn't been able to get enough of him. Had the fact that he'd taken a business call instead of engaging in some sort of post-coital conversation done it?

No, her hostility towards him was all about the business. He'd usurped her authority. And she was right—pleasurable as it had been, Saturday night was of no consequence. As she was the centre's most senior staff member, he needed her support if he was going to keep Aussie Essential. Somehow he had to get Kate the employee onside.

Somewhere away from the office environment might work. A peace offering. Food. Did she like pizza? he wondered.

Kate could see the door from her desk and let out a relieved sigh when she saw Damon Gillespie's broad shoulders as he exited the room and headed to the rear of the building. Could the day get any worse? She closed her eyes. Yeah, it *could* have been worse.

He could have recognised her.

Bryce's nephew.

Perhaps her soon-to-be boss, if his take-charge attitude was any indication. A man she despised for all the right reasons—a selfish jet-setter about to snatch the manager's job out from under her.

So why did the sight of him melt her insides to butter? Why couldn't she get *over* him? The man who'd just taken charge wasn't the fantasy lover she'd had on Saturday night. Somehow she had to separate her professional and personal life, which had suddenly become hopelessly entangled.

She rubbed a hand over her throbbing head. Despite his

lackadaisical lifestyle she had a feeling Damon Gillespie was a very astute man—how long would it be before he discovered who she was?

# CHAPTER THREE

KATE was about to microwave last night's left-over chicken soup for tea, hoping she could somehow manage to put something in her stomach, when her phone rang.

'Kate.'

'Yes…' She couldn't say anything more because her heart leapt into her throat at the sound of his already familiar voice. It was as if he were right there, murmuring in her ear. She could almost feel his breath on her skin; the heat seemed to shimmer through the connection. What did he want? she thought distractedly. Ah…he'd said he'd be contacting her about the list of people who'd attended the funeral.

'How's the cold?'

'Improving.' Actually she felt much better after an extra dose of pills and a couple of hours' nap. She glanced at the clock and her voice held an accusatory tone as she said, 'It's half past eight, Mr Gillespie. Work's over.'

'I know, I meant to call earlier. I hope you're hungry.'

Her stomach churned. Surely he wasn't inviting her out for dinner? She looked down at her worn black tracksuit pants under the oversize orange nightshirt, the fluffy pink slippers she'd meant to replace last winter. 'No, I'm not. I take it you're ringing about the list,' she hurried on. 'I'll bring it tomorr—'

'You have to eat, Kate. Did you have lunch?'

'No, I…' She was interrupted—no, *saved*—by the sound of knocking at her door and breathed a little sigh of relief at the interruption. 'I have to go, I have a visitor, I'll ring you back in a bit.' When it was late and she could lie and say she'd already eaten. If she rang back at all…

She dropped the phone onto its base, hurried through the living room and dragged open the door. 'Oh…'

Damon Gillespie. With his mobile still attached to his ear. Wearing khaki cargo pants and a white T-shirt tonight and balancing a pizza box and a small package in his spare hand. He disconnected the phone with his thumb, slipped it into his pocket, all without taking his eyes off hers. 'Hi.'

His gaze flicked down to the fluffy slippers and her toes curled up in embarrassment. And she'd been too distracted to slip something over her nightshirt; her braless breasts—the breasts he'd handled with such expertise—jutted out at him. 'I wasn't expecting anyone,' she muttered.

His eyes flashed with amusement. 'You were keen enough to answer the door a second or two ago.'

'No… I thought it was my sister…' But he saw through her, she just knew it. She didn't want to share pizza with him, she didn't want him in her home, checking out her state of dishabille, but what choice did she have? Too late to dive for cover now. She turned away and began heading back to the kitchen. 'Come in, but I'm telling you now I couldn't eat pizza if my life depended on it.'

'Ah, but you haven't tried Dominic Amigo's Gourmet Pizza, have you?'

Her brows rose. 'Have *you*? I thought you just rolled into town?'

'Sandy recommended it when I rang this afternoon for your contact details and we got talking about local restaurants. You were with a customer at the time.'

'Remind me to thank her,' she murmured as she pulled plates from her cupboard and searched out a spatula. She tried to ignore the pizza's tempting aroma, but it did smell good and her stomach rumbled in spite of herself. In the silence it sounded more like a blocked drain clearing.

'Not hungry, huh?' He set the box down on the tiny glass-topped table, pulled out a chair and grinned.

She hadn't seen that grin since Saturday night. A bone-meltingly sexy grin that turned her insides to mush and made her do crazy, stupid, reckless things.

Like having sex with a complete stranger.

Forcing her gaze away from him, she looked at the other item he'd brought. 'What's in the bag?'

'Fresh ginger root and a couple of essential oils—peppermint and tea tree. Grandma used to swear by them when Bry and I had colds. I've written the instructions out; they're inside the bag.'

He'd thought enough to bring her a family cold remedy? A warm feeling of…something—like *maybe* she'd misjudged him?—seeped into her bones, going some way to melting the frost. She didn't know what to say. 'That's very kind. Thanks.'

'You're welcome.'

She withdrew the items along with the handwritten note. Firm, bold, decisive writing. It denoted someone who was confident and at ease with himself. 'You still use it, then?'

'I never get a cold. In fact I'm disgustingly healthy.'

Yes. She could see that. She turned away from the unsettling sight of his more-than-healthy masculinity and peered in the fridge to cool her rapidly heating face and to search for something to offer to drink.

'Ah, two plates,' he said. 'Does that mean you've decided to join me?'

'If it's got olives I could be tempted.' And if anyone could tempt her… In any way…

It would *not* be Damon Gillespie.

'There's mozzarella cheese, marinated roasted chicken,

capsicum, mushrooms, onion with fresh coriander smothered in satay sauce. No olives.'

'Satay chicken. I never heard of satay chicken pizza. You sure you didn't stop in at Nonja's Rasa Sayang and forget the fried rice on your way out?'

'You'll love it.'

She retrieved an unopened bottle and held it up. 'Is sparkling mineral water okay?'

'Fine.'

'Okay. We can talk while we eat.' That way she could kill two birds with one stone and get him out of her apartment sooner. She set two glasses down, filled them, then sank down on the only other chair.

'Sure we can, but not about business.' He lifted the lid and inhaled appreciatively. 'Not while we're eating pizza.' He slid a slice of the delicious-smelling food onto a plate and pushed it towards her. 'Now, eat.'

She did as he asked and was surprised to find how hungry she was. Having food in her stomach also put her in a slightly better frame of mind. 'I expect this has all been a bolt out of the blue,' she said after a few moments. She thought she saw something like grief flicker in his eyes before he deliberately snuffed it out. A thread of surprise wound through her.

'Who'd expect a forty-three-year-old guy with no history of illness to drop dead with no warning?' He returned his attention to the pizza, sliding out another piece for himself as he said, 'It's a blow losing the only family you have left.'

She couldn't begin to imagine losing her family. They were the most important thing to her. 'Your parents…?'

His expression changed, the lines around his mouth deepened, the golden colour of his eyes, moments ago so bright and alive, dulled. 'I've no idea where they are. Haven't seen or heard from them in years. Gran raised me alongside Bryce. Dad won't know his only brother's died because I didn't know how to contact him. Even if I'd wanted to.'

The bitterness in the rough-throated voice stunned Kate. She realised she'd been so caught up in the injustice of Damon's apparent takeover at Aussie Essential and his appearance in her kitchen, she hadn't really given him much of a chance. 'I'm s—'

'Don't.' Damon held up a hand and mentally shook himself. What the hell was he doing, giving Kate Fielding a glimpse of his vulnerability? The part that he kept private and ruthlessly hidden. He'd rid himself of his anger and self-pity years ago. Buried it under a mountain of hard work and harder play.

He turned his attention to lifting the pizza to his mouth. Its spicy, succulent flavours slid over his tongue, pleasure danced across his taste buds. He hadn't tasted a pizza like it anywhere in the world. 'The food's good, don't you think?'

A tiny frown still marred her brow, as if she didn't quite believe he could be so dismissive of his inner pain.

'Try something for me,' he said. 'Bite off a mouthful, chew it slowly and concentrate.' Anything to distract her from probing into his history.

She hesitated, then raised another slice to her lips. He watched her take a bite and savour it a moment, her eyes half closed. It sent a trickle of heat to his groin. Then she licked her lips, leaving a glossy sheen of oil clinging to them. 'It's good,' she agreed.

The trickle of heat grew. Tonight she looked different yet again. More accessible than the closed businesswoman he'd seen this morning, and yet, perversely, there'd been something about that buttoned-up image that had turned him on. He couldn't stop himself imagining her sprawled on that big desk right now. While he slipped off her jacket, popped the buttons on her blouse and pulled down her bra… The trickle turned to a torrent.

Then there was Shakira—masked and mysterious but blatantly sexy with plenty of cleavage and smooth bare skin. That intriguing ruby glittering in her navel. He couldn't help but wonder if she still wore it, whether it was attached to her somehow, like a body piercing.

And now the informal look. Very informal. But no less tantalising for all that. For a start she'd let her hair down. It cascaded halfway down her back, a waterfall of shiny black silk that begged for his touch. In her nightshirt she was obviously ready for bed.

*Don't go there,* he warned himself as an image of Kate and heat and sheets rose before him. The nightshirt proclaimed in glittery letters that diamonds were a girl's best friend. 'Is that a personal motto?' He waved his pizza slice towards her chest.

She stopped mid-bite and as he watched two little buds rose beneath the fabric. 'What?'

'You'd go for money over men?'

She frowned, looked down and her expression cleared. 'It's just a nightshirt, for heaven's sake.' But her eyes met his in a challenge. 'When—or if—I find a man who's worth more I'll let you know. On second thought, I won't bother, since you probably won't be here for me to tell you anyway. Where did you say you live again?'

'Wherever I happen to be working.' Or pursuing his various recreational activities.

'And what exactly is your line of work?'

He shrugged, evasive. 'I take on whatever comes my way.'

Aware of her disapproval, and satisfied with it somehow, he lifted his glass, took a long slow drink. He didn't stay anywhere long. Nor did he feel inclined to talk about it.

His own motto: *Make your success, have your fun, and move on. Don't make attachments—with people or places.* Which made his Internet-based business so attractive. He set his glass down and resumed his demolition of the pizza without speaking.

'And yet you want to take on a travel agency.' Her lips pursed, then parted as she picked up another slice of pizza. Damn, he wanted to taste that mouth again. He wanted *her* again, all of her—even in tracksuit pants and nightshirt. Or without them. And he could tell by the tension crackling between them earlier today and now that the attraction was mutual.

But she didn't *like* him, he thought, staring into those hostile eyes as they both continued to eat.

She seemed like the kind of woman who wanted to take on responsibility. Focused, career-oriented, the kind who lived for work. Maybe she was only looking for temporary in a relationship too. After all, how many women carried a condom in their skirts? 'You like cooking?' he asked, diverting her thoughts, wanting to thaw the frosty edge to her mood.

'It depends. If I'm having company over, I like trying out different things. But I hate the boredom of cooking for one day in, day out.'

'Ever try cooking for Bryce?' he said wryly. 'Never knew a less adventurous eater. Same old meat and three veg every day. At least he did last time I saw him.'

'Yeah, I know.' A tiny smile curved her lips as she wiped her mouth on a paper napkin and pushed her plate to the side.

Ah, she was warming. He leaned back and smiled too. 'So, do you do much travelling with your job?'

'I go overseas once a year and do a few interstate famils— what we in the industry call familiarisation tours. Bryce had promised me I could do something a little more adventurous this year.'

'Adventurous. Would that be along the lines of trekking Nepal?' He popped the last piece of pizza into his mouth and reached for a napkin.

'Heavens, no, nothing like that.' A half-laugh bubbled out. 'Roughing it is not my kind of holiday. I'm more of a five-star luxury girl.'

'An overseas nightclub tour, then? Sampling the hottest spots in town?'

'Nightclubbing really isn't my scene.' She stacked their

plates. 'I'm more of a family person. I usually spend my evenings at home or with my sister. Mostly.'

The last word was spoken in a subtly different tone, as if she was remembering evenings when family was the last thing on her mind.

'So there are times when you give yourself permission to let your hair down, so to speak.'

Almost panicked eyes darted to his, so wide, so dark her irises seemed to disappear into her pupils. 'Of course. Doesn't everyone?' The frost was back in her voice as she rose abruptly, disposed of the plates in the sink and shoved the pizza box beside a swing-top bin, her movements swift and jerky.

She produced a sponge and wiped it over the table. 'Okay, meal's done.' She flicked her eyes to him. 'Shall we get started?'

All kinds of scenarios of how they could get started smoked through his mind. Beginning with lifting her nightshirt and finding out about that ruby once and for all. Then he'd slide his hands through her silken hair, bring those bare, kissable lips to his and...

'Here's the funeral attendees' book.' Her brisk voice broke his train of thought as she slapped it on the table. She reached for some handwritten notes stuck to the fridge with a souvenir magnet from San Francisco. She sat down again, spreading the papers in front of her. 'These are the people you might want to thank. They're mostly business associates.'

He had to ask. 'You said you two were friends, Kate. What did that mean?'

She raised her eyes to his. 'Exactly what it sounds like. We used to have a kind of standing date for Friday nights,' she continued after a moment. 'We talked over the week's business in more pleasant surroundings. Our relationship was only ever purely professional.'

He nodded, somehow relieved. 'Let me guess—same time, same place?'

She let out a half-laugh. 'Yes.'

He nodded. That was good old Bryce—predictable.

'It saved time.' She shrugged. 'I knew him a long while.'

By the time they were done more than an hour had passed. Kate had been conscious of Damon's molten amber gaze on her all evening. It made her wonder if it was because he recognised her from Saturday night. It certainly wasn't for the wild look she was wearing this evening. But she could hardly ask him about it, could she?

Without looking at him she shuffled her notes into a tidy pile. 'Here you go.'

'Thanks.'

He reached across the table and put a hand on hers. A sparkle of heat shot up her arm but before she could pull it away his fingers were stroking her wrist, his thumb rasping over the pulse point that suddenly beat like a drum.

She forced her eyes to his. 'I hope it helps.' Her neck prickled with heat. 'The information, I mean.'

'I know what you mean.' He smiled. He still had hold of her hand.

She didn't move. He hadn't touched her—deliberately touched her, unless she counted the restraining hand this morning—since Saturday night. His eyes looked right into hers and for a moment she thought he was going to remind her of that, but instead he withdrew his hand.

'I'd better be off and let you get some sleep,' he said, and pushed up. 'Don't forget to try the oils.'

'I won't. Thank you.'

He nodded, then turned and walked to her door. 'I won't be in tomorrow morning. I've got to see the solicitor and sort through Bryce's stuff.'

She couldn't resist a terse, 'I'm sure we'll manage without you.'

He grinned. 'I'm sure you will. Kate…' his grin sobered '…you've been doing a great job there. Thank you.'

She needed to say, *had* to say, 'Bryce intended making me manager. Next month.'

'He was leaving?'

'I don't know what he intended. He hadn't told me anything more than he was taking some time off.'

Damon's brows drew together. 'We've got some decisions to make. I'll need your staffing knowledge and expertise.'

What the heck did *that* mean? At this point all she could do was nod a reluctant acceptance.

'Good night, Kate.' He hesitated on the step.

His cologne teased her nostrils. Oh, my God, was he going to kiss her? She didn't realise she'd stepped back until his bronze eyes flashed in the reflected light from the hall. 'What's wrong?'

'Nothing.'

His eyes narrowed, as if he was trying to figure her out. He was being a gentleman, unlike the bad boy she'd experienced Saturday night, making it hard for her to reconcile the two. Or more like he was just being the businessman and she was the only one with sex on her mind.

A flush rose to her cheeks and she tucked her hands beneath her armpits. 'Goodnight.'

She closed the door the moment he left and leaned back against it. She heard a car door shut, the smooth purr of a well-tuned engine, then listened as the sound faded.

Only then did she breathe the sigh she'd held inside for the past few moments. He'd been nice this evening, not the take-charge guy in the office this morning. He'd brought her pizza and his grandma's recipe. What kind of man thought to bring a girl he barely knew something like that? Something of himself. The same kind who'd have sex with a girl he didn't know?

But men could compartmentalise their lives. Especially where sex was concerned. She only had to think of her ex-fiancé. She'd never trust a man again. Nor did she think she could trust her own judgement again. One mistake was enough.

But it was kind of sad to think that Damon would be on his own tonight. She couldn't imagine having no family, no support through the tough times. Even if her dad was over-bearing and treated her as if she were sixteen rather than thirty, she could forgive him because she knew he'd do anything for her. Damon had none of that.

But she needed to remember—he was the boss she'd had a one-night stand with—which left her in a precarious position.

She was sure he hadn't recognised her. Thank goodness for that; she was safe for now. And yet, instead of being relieved, perversely, the knowledge somehow disappointed her.

Bryce's apartment was on the outskirts of the city's business district. Damon spent the following morning cleaning up. He did a quick inventory, then went grocery shopping for a few essentials.

By midday he sat at the cramped, overloaded desk in Bry's home office. He'd been at it for more than an hour, trying—and failing—to find some logical order to the shoeboxes brimming with papers. He pulled out an overdue electricity account from the top of one, let it fall back on the desk. He had no doubt Bry ran his business the same way.

Hell.

He massaged the stiffness at the back of his neck, then scrubbed a hand over his face. His eyes felt sandy. His jaw ached from clenching his teeth. It was interrupted sleep, that was what it was. Caused by the woman who'd taken up resi-dence inside his head. It had taken all his will power last night not to kiss Kate.

He'd made love to her. The most beguiling woman he'd ever seen. The most responsive woman he'd ever had. She'd fulfilled his every fantasy with her sultry mystery, and that erotic ruby glitter in her belly button. The way she'd come undone at his touch, her unrestrained abandon.

It had been a charade; Sha-ki-ra really was a fantasy. Kate

Fielding's alter ego. Fascinating. Who'd have thought straight-down-the-line Kate from the agency's office liked to play?

The question that interested him was did she play by the same rules he did?

# CHAPTER FOUR

KATE arrived at work early on Tuesday just in case Damon changed his mind and turned up unexpectedly. No way was she going to let him see she wasn't up to the job. She switched on her computer and called up one of yesterday's files.

Last night she'd used the oils he'd given her and indulged in a hot, fragrant bath. Whether it was the fantasy of imagining him sharing it with her, the knowledge that Damon had given her the oils, or his grandmother's recipe, she'd felt amazing afterwards. Revived, refreshed.

Didn't mean she felt any less resentment towards him this morning. Today it was back to business. Business and recreation were separate entities. *Say it again, business and recreation are sep—*

'So, what do you think?' Sandy's voice interrupted her inner lecture.

Kate glanced up from her computer, took one look at the dreamy expression on her colleague's face and knew what Sandy meant. Still, she said, 'About what?'

'The new boss. Damon.'

The way she said his name, like a sigh, grated on Kate's nerves. Not the way a staff member should talk about a potential employer, Kate thought with a primness that surprised even her.

'He's not strictly our boss, Sandy.' Kate resumed tapping

keys, suddenly aware of a prickly heat beneath the front of her crisp white blouse. 'Not until he says he's our boss. He hasn't told us what he's decided yet. He might sell.'

'But he's already making changes.'

Kate stopped typing and stared at her. 'Changes?'

'Don't tell me you haven't noticed the new state-of-the-art whiz-bang coffee machine in the lunch room?'

Coffee machine? When had that been delivered? Where did he think the money for that was coming from, for heaven's sake? Not the social-club funds. 'I haven't had time for coffee. I've this group booking to finalise and the airline's giving me the runaround. Anyway, we don't need a coffee machine,' she muttered.

'What's with you?' Sandy frowned at Kate over her computer monitor. 'You've been nothing but snarly with him. You got something against drop-dead gorgeous?'

'No. If you go for that rugged outdoorsy type.' Kate resumed studying her computer screen without really seeing it, but looked up again as something occurred to her. 'You didn't tell me he phoned me yesterday afternoon.'

'Oh. I forgot. Sorry.'

'You told him I was with a customer. I didn't have any customers. I worked out back because I didn't want to infect anyone with my sniffles.'

Sandy shrugged, a half-baked smile on her face. 'Guess I was mistaken. Sorry again.' She bounced up off her chair. 'Let me make it up to you. I'll make you the best coffee you ever had. It even makes cappuccino—'

'No!' Kate snapped. 'No,' she said again, striving for the calm professionalism she was known for, which seemed to have deserted her this week. 'Thanks, I'll get one myself in a while.' *Drop-dead gorgeous* was already the cause of office conflict and he hadn't been here more than forty-eight hours.

Coffee machine! She scoffed to herself as she punched in the airline's number yet again and was put on hold. It was obvious he was trying to lure the staff onto his side. Sandy was already there. They'd like him, they'd *want* him to stay. Where would that leave her?

And what next after the coffee machine? An Under New Management sign on the window and a change in name? Damon Gillespie looked like the kind of man who'd want to make his own mark on the business. She could just picture 'Damon's Travel' up there in big red letters.

Regular customers came here because they trusted Aussie Essential. Personalised service with a smile, the best deals around—somehow Bryce had always managed to undercut the competition. Why change something that worked?

She'd just finalised the booking from hell when her phone rang again. 'Good morning, Aussie Essential Travel, Kate Fielding speaking. How can I help you?'

'And good morning to you, too, Kate. Glad to hear you're sounding better today.'

No name—of course a man like him would expect her to recognise his voice. She was tempted to play dumb but he'd know, damn him. 'Damon.' Her own professional voice slid a notch, her pulse stepped up one. She shot a quick glance at Sandy. Thankfully she was busy on her own phone. 'What can I do for you?'

A pause while he considered her offer. She swore the connection crackled with the possibilities.

'I'd like to use your local knowledge this afternoon,' he said, finally. 'Can you make yourself available at three?'

'I… Is this work-related?'

'Of course.'

By the tone in his voice she could almost hear him saying, *What else would it be?*

What else indeed. She knew he was attracted to her; he just didn't know they'd already had sex. And he wasn't getting another chance—Kate Fielding, *employee*, was off limits. 'I think I can clear my schedule.'

'Good. I'll pick you up.'

As in they were going somewhere? 'Is it just the two of us?'

'Yes. Does that bother you?'

*Yes.* 'No. Of course not.'

'Business hours are from eight forty-five to five-thirty, Kate. Anything else…' He let the sentence hang. A long-drawn-out hiatus.

Oh. Lord. Her heart turned over in her chest as every female cell in her body begged. It was the *anything else* that bothered her.

She cleared a huskiness from her throat. 'Fine.'

'Okay, see you in a while.'

Tugging off her phone headset, she sagged back against her chair feeling as if she'd run the Sydney marathon. She hoped they were through whatever it was they were doing by five-thirty. After hours was too damn dangerous.

Kate shut down her computer and grabbed her bag the moment she saw Damon climbing out of a silver BMW in front of the office. For reasons she didn't care to think about she didn't want Damon greeting her with an audience hanging on their every word.

'Any problems, Sandy, ring my mobile,' she said on her way past.

'Try to be nice,' Sandy suggested. 'We want to keep him.'

A cool wind with the scent of rain greeted her as she stepped outside. Damon cast a lingering glance over her professional black pant-suit and white blouse, almost a duplicate of his black leather jacket, white open-necked shirt and casual trousers, then grinned as he opened the passenger door. 'Perfect match.'

He waited while she slid onto the seat and swung her legs inside, then closed the door.

She gave him the same once-over as he rounded the

bonnet. Yes—unfortunately they coordinated like a couple who'd dressed in sync. The image of them sharing a bedroom and selecting clothes together sent a wave of heat through her. 'I thought it was my local expertise you needed,' she said as he switched on the ignition and the car purred into life.

'And so it is. We'll be walking a bit if the weather holds; I hope you're wearing comfortable shoes.'

'You know I am.' He'd had a good long look at her low-heeled, comfortable shoes. *Grandma shoes.* A hip problem she'd had since birth made wearing the feminine high heels she longed for an impossibility if she didn't want to endure the pain and discomfort it entailed. She changed the subject. 'Expensive car you're driving. You're renting it while you're here?' Or was he spending up on his inheritance already?

'Leased it. Looks like I'll be staying a while. I have to wind up Bry's estate and then there's the business.'

'Yes. The business.' Her job depended on Damon and what he decided to do. The promotion she'd worked for was slipping frustratingly beyond her reach.

A hand touched hers briefly, but his eyes remained on the road. 'You're very quiet. Is everything okay?'

The warmth of those callused fingers, the memory of that hand on other body parts, had her edging away with a tight-lipped, 'This is supposed to be a work-related exercise.'

The tension inside the car ratcheted up. From the corner of her eye she saw him shake his head. No doubt after this assignment he'd think her the humourless strait-laced virgin type. Which was a *good* thing, she told herself. She looked straight ahead, trying not to notice the scent of his body-warmed leather jacket, the sound it made as he shifted in his seat.

It began to rain, one of those quick downpours that sent pedestrians scurrying for shelter and umbrellas and was over in moments. Damon parked beside a playground a short distance from a travel agency two blocks over from Aussie Essential.

'Let's start here,' he said, handing her a pad and pen. 'I want you to take note of their special offers, prices, et cetera. We need to know what others in the area are doing in order to remain competitive.'

'For heaven's sakes, Bryce was always very competitive. And all we have to do is look on their websites.'

'You get a better idea looking at the sorts of customers they attract, the general layout of the shop, the surrounding businesses.'

'You don't need me for that.' She frowned at him. 'You could've done this on your own.'

He grinned. 'But it wouldn't have been half as much fun.'

Turning to the window, she ignored the way his eyes twinkled at her, the way her body responded to his proximity, and watched the light rain trickle down the window, turning the streetscape into ragged water-colour impressions. 'We'll be arrested for loitering.'

Hopefully that was all they'd be arrested for because it was taking more and more will power not to slide closer and feel how soft and pliable that leather jacket was. How hard and warm the flesh beneath it felt…

'What are you thinking, Kate?'

Oh, no. She was not going there. 'I'm thinking I can't even read the signage from here.'

'That's what binoculars are for.' He reached into the glovebox.

'The windscreen's fogging up and we'll be arrested for stalking as well. *Enough.*' She turned to him, furious with herself for agreeing to accompany him on this farcical exercise. Furious with Damon for thinking she was gullible enough to. 'What the hell's this all about?'

The humour faded from his eyes, turning them to the colour of dark honey. 'Okay. I wanted to talk to you. Just you. On our own.'

She went very still while every internal organ swapped

places. 'You got me here under false pretences,' she said, tight-lipped. 'You don't want to check out the competition. You want…'

She looked away, unable to look at him, to let him see what he surely must read on her face, and rubbed at the misty windscreen with a ferocious hand. Lemon sunlight was breaking through the light drizzle, filling the air outside with a misty quality.

'I *want* your honest opinion about where Aussie Travel's going. I didn't want the rest of the staff listening in on the conversation.'

Oh. He wasn't here to seduce her. His mind was on *work*. Good. She told herself that was *good*. She let her pent-up breath out in tiny increments, directing her focus to the matter at hand. 'Everything seems okay,' she said slowly. 'Except the books. Bryce always did the accounting side of things himself. But since he passed away I've been looking them over and I can't make any sense of them. I'm no accountant, but we need to get someone in who knows what they're doing.'

Damon frowned. 'Yeah. Asap.' He'd only had time to glance at last month's sales figures yesterday—what he could find of them at short notice—and they didn't match with the banking statements. He met her eyes directly. 'I'll be straight with you, Kate. Aussie Essential needs a hell of a lot of work.'

'You've looked at the finances?' Kate's eyebrows rose.

'Does that surprise you?'

She wrinkled her forehead. 'Frankly… Yes.'

'Your opinion of me isn't very high.'

Her complexion turned pink as she stared straight ahead. 'I don't know you well enough to form an opinion.'

He reached for her chin, turned her so that she had no choice but to face him. So that he could see the subtle changes in those deeper-than-midnight eyes. 'Based on what you do know, Kate.'

'You already told me you don't stay in one place for long. So my guess is you don't stick at something and see it through.'

Something deeper flickered in her eyes, prompting him to say, 'Go on.'

'You take your pleasure where you find it.'

Ah. Pleasure. An immediate image of Kate flared in his mind. 'You mean women? I thought you only wanted to concentrate on business?'

She shrugged, her eyes darting away. 'I'm interested in whatever impacts on the business.' Then she seemed to find some inner strength and gave him the full measure of her gaze. 'You tire of something and move on. Am I right?'

His grip on her chin loosened and it was his turn to look away as he fought the darkness that had plagued him for too many years. 'Some might make that assumption.'

'Why will it be different this time?'

'This is my uncle's business. Now my business.' He looked back at her. 'You don't want me here, do you?'

Her lack of response was the only answer he needed. Not that he expected one. It wasn't so much a question as a statement of fact. And yet they'd had sex. Wild, out-of-control, satisfying sex. The best sex he'd ever had.

And she knew it. She just didn't know he did. Time to fess up.

Damon ran a hand inside the neck of his shirt to rid himself of the sensation that he was strangling. There was too much intensity in this damn car. The conversation had gone way beyond what he'd expected. His own fault. He pushed open the car door. 'Let's take a walk.'

'But it's raining,' she said, chewing on her lip.

He looked away from the perfection of her mouth and its lush temptation. 'It's soft rain, barely there. Live a little.'

The playground was empty, the trees weeping moisture, diamonds winking in the weak sunlight. Damon swept the wetness away from a swing with his hand and lowered himself, its worn wooden seat barely big enough, and set it in motion.

Kate stood on the grass, her suit jacket neatly buttoned, her hair perfectly swept up into a clasp. Tiny beads of moisture glistened amongst the dark strands. He could read her expression and it screamed disapproval. She looked so out of place he couldn't help but grin. 'Come on, Ms Fielding, there're two swings.'

She glanced at her watch. 'We're wasting time.'

'Is it a waste of time if you're doing something you enjoy?'

'You might be enjoying this childish behaviour.' She waved a hand. 'I, on the other hand, am not.'

'Because you're not allowing yourself to.'

She looked down at her business attire, then the swing and shook her head. 'The seat's wet.'

'Easily remedied.' He stood, shrugged out of his leather jacket and laid it on the swing seat. When she still didn't move, he jogged over to her. 'Be childish for a few moments.' He grabbed her hand, felt its cool smoothness as he met her eyes. 'You know you want to.'

She hesitated before acquiescing and letting him tug her towards the swings. She sat down on his jacket, a tiny smile kicking up at the corner of her mouth as she pushed off. 'I haven't done this since I was twelve.'

He sat beside her and matched his swing to hers. For a few moments they moved in harmony with the memories of childhood; the creak of the swing and the shift of air against their faces, the squeal of excited kids as a couple strolled through the far gate with their young family in tow.

'You're worried about your job,' he said. 'Don't be.'

'Easy for you to say. Your income isn't on the line. If what you say is true, we're in a whole lot of trouble. And it's not just me. There are six of us depending on work.'

So he'd dig them out; it was what he did best. Before he moved on to another challenge. But he didn't want staff knowing he'd have to invest a sizeable amount more of his own capital just to keep their heads above water. 'I'll do everything I can to keep you all in work.'

She nodded. 'Fair enough. All you can do is try.' Checking her watch, she said, 'Speaking of work, I have a lot of it to do before I go home this evening.' The pleasure that had crept into her eyes and pinkened her cheeks dimmed.

It deflated his own mood. He'd enjoyed watching that sparkle. He hadn't seen it since Saturday night. 'The boss won't mind if you take a break.'

She reined in the swing, stood and stepped away. 'You're not my boss. You haven't said you've committed to the business long term yet and our conversation has given me reason to think otherwise. You might help us for a while, then up and disappear.'

'You think I'd do that?'

She shrugged. 'I don't really know you.'

'Well, then, a good reason to loiter together in the playground a little longer,' he said. But she wasn't listening. He swiped up his jacket and followed the rigid line of her back as she headed towards the car.

On their way back a sudden impulse had him turning off his intended route to the office. He headed instead for Diamond Bay, north of Bondi where the surf and rocks were a world away from the cityscape of Sydney's CBD.

'Where are we going?' she said with a frown.

'I want to show you something.'

He parked where they could see the cliffs and the Pacific Ocean rolling in. Grey and misty today but no less wild in its beauty. He climbed out, walked a few paces, breathing in the familiar salt-spray scent while he waited for Kate to follow. The sound of the waves crashing below echoed in his ears. 'This used to be my favourite place when I was growing up,' he said when she stood beside him.

'You lived round here?' she said, gazing at the homes nearby.

'No.' He shrugged deeper inside his jacket as a sudden chill gust blew over them. 'We lived in a semi-industrial part of town where the trains rattled our windows and vibrated through the floor night and day. This was our escape.'

'You and Bryce?'

'Not Bryce.' He narrowed his eyes against the sting of the wind, annoyed with his slip of the tongue. 'We'd walk for miles, following the cliff top. Sometimes we'd dodge beneath the railing and see who could stand the closest to the edge.'

'No way!' He felt her incredulous gaze on his face. 'How old were you?'

He continued looking out to sea where a rainstorm was sweeping in, watching gulls swoop and dive. He'd always envied them their freedom. 'Twelve, I guess.'

'So I played on swings while you risked your neck.'

'Yeah.' The last time he'd been here had been the day after Bonita had succumbed to leukaemia. He'd looked out at the horizon and wondered where she was now, then down at the unforgiving rocks below. And briefly considered the unthinkable…

It was the day he'd vowed to live for today and never look back.

'It's a long way to fall,' Kate said quietly, following his gaze.

He crossed his arms against the cold, fighting melancholy. Coming here to his and Bonita's favourite spot had been a mistake. Bringing Kate had been a bigger one. And yet, somehow, with Kate at his side, he felt soothed. It was almost as if she shared his sadness.

What did she know about losing someone? He had no idea. He didn't want to know because it meant sharing his pain and he wasn't willing to open himself up to that.

It started to rain in earnest. 'Time to go,' he said, grabbing her hand, holding it a moment against him, her life force seeping through his shirt as comforting as a glass of warm milk while rain lashed their faces. Her eyes brimmed with moisture—as if she, too, knew of loss—and were full of soul.

If he looked deeper, he might even see his own reflected there.

He relinquished his hold as quickly as he'd taken it and stepped away. No. He risked his body and his life for the pure adrenaline rush and he did it several times a year. The only risks he was willing to take didn't involve his heart.

# CHAPTER FIVE

'HAVE dinner with me,' Damon said. They were back in his car and on the way home. He'd already phoned Sandy, told her they weren't coming back and asked her to close up.

Kate glanced at his tense jaw, shadowed with a hint of sexy stubble. Sexy, she could do without, but there was no hint of romantic intention in his voice, just the quiet tone of a friend in need of company.

Except…today was Tuesday, the evening she visited her family. Up there on the cliffs she'd forgotten. She too had been thinking of another time. When her brother had died in a hang-glider accident on the side of a mountain. 'I go to my parents' house for tea every Tuesday.'

'*Every* Tuesday?' He glanced her way, then shrugged a shoulder and returned his eyes to the road. 'No worries. Your family comes first—it's no big deal.'

But Kate heard the thread of disappointment running through his words. Something had happened on the cliff top, to both of them. Something that went deeper than sex or attraction. It had left her shaken. With her track record, she should be running for the hills, but instead she heard herself say, 'I'll phone them and put it off.'

'Not necessary.'

Ignoring him, she pulled out her mobile, but got the answering service. 'Mum, hi. I'm not going to make it tonight.

I'm having tea with…Bryce's nephew. We have some work to finish. Sorry for the late notice, I'll call you later.'

She disconnected, aware that Damon had been listening—how could he not?—and that she hadn't used his name. Was that her mind's way of distancing herself from him? she wondered. She didn't want her parents knowing too much about Damon. She didn't think she could talk about him and not blush. He'd also heard her lie about working tonight. Did he think she had to lie to her family, that she couldn't make her own decisions? 'Um, there's a little place not far from—'

'Let me cook.'

'Oh.' She'd expected to be eating in a restaurant. She hadn't considered that there'd be just the two of them. Alone. Her pulse skipped a beat, but she kept her voice steady and conversational. 'You cook?'

'I love to eat, which means I have to cook. I'm pretty good at it.' A corner of his mouth tipped up as he glanced at her. 'But I'd like your opinion.'

'If you're expecting to cook at my place, I haven't been shopping…'

'That's okay, I stocked up this morning. We'll eat at Bry's.' He looked at her again. 'You okay with that?'

'Yes. Of course.'

Damon turned down the next side street, switched directions and headed for Bryce's apartment. He'd half expected to have to cajole her into it, but she'd accepted, cancelled her usual family meal no less, even though her stiff affirmative suggested she wasn't altogether comfortable with the idea.

He wanted to reach out and touch her and not have her pull away from him as she had this afternoon with her coolly formal excuse that their excursion was work-related. Her business side. Where was the flirty girl he remembered from Saturday night?

He could smell her exotic summer perfume. Frangipani. Keeping quiet about it wasn't doing him any favours. He wanted what they'd shared out in the open: the most spectacular sex he'd ever had. With the most enchanting woman he'd ever seen. He wanted to move on from there, not start again. He wanted to see more of uninhibited Shakira. A lot more.

He should have told her he knew who she was right off. Should have known the moment he clapped eyes on her again at the staff meeting that their one night wasn't going to be the end of it. He could play along, attempt to win 'straight Kate' over without ever mentioning that evening, or he could come clean.

Tonight.

His body tightened at the thought. 'Shakira' couldn't deny the attraction as Kate might. There'd be no secrets between them, no barriers. Just the acknowledgement that they'd shared something fantastic. And could do again.

But, perhaps more than the fevered anticipation of getting properly naked with her, tonight he wanted her company. Gut instinct told him she wanted that too. Whether he was dealing with business, sports or the female population, he'd always trusted his gut and it had never let him down.

Twenty minutes later he had the wine breathing and a green salad in the making. Kate had taken off her damp suit jacket while he'd changed into dry cargo pants and T-shirt, leaving his feet bare. She seemed to be having a hard time doing nothing and, since he couldn't suggest what he'd like her to be doing with those restless hands, he'd given her the task of buttering bread.

'I hope you like fish,' he said, taking a couple of Atlantic salmon cutlets from the fridge. He drizzled them with olive oil, adding pepper, capers and chopped capsicum, herbs.

'I do.'

Her mobile buzzed and she licked her fingers before diving into her bag. 'Hi, Rosa. Ah…' She turned away and walked to the door that led onto the patio, slid it open and stepped outside. 'No, that's a bad idea. I hardly know him, Rose,' she said sotto voce, unaware Damon could hear her through the open kitchen window.

Damon pulled out fixings for a lemon-based salad dressing and set the frying pan on the hotplate while the one-sided conversation continued.

'No. He's not the kind of guy you bring home to meet Mum and Dad, okay? Even if he does look the part in a suit and tie—when he bothers to wear it. Underneath that polished veneer…' A pause. A breathy laugh. 'Yeah, exactly. Hey, don't you dare tell Mum…'

*Tell Mum what?* He could only guess what Rosa had said that made Kate respond in that breathy way. Probably meant they were talking dirty. She was remembering Saturday night. His hand tightened on the bottle he was holding. Images associated with the conversation were likely to result in acute discomfort.

'Anyway, there's no point,' Kate went on. 'He's only here to finalise everything, sort out whatever he wants to do with the business—sell it, presumably—then he'll be gone. Who knows whether I'll even have a job next month? Listen, I have to go. Ciao.'

A few seconds later she returned, set her phone on the bench and resumed buttering bread with a vengeance, head bent, eyes on her task.

Damon slid the cutlets into the pan. The sizzle and aroma of frying capsicum and fresh herbs filled the air. While that was cooking he tossed the salad and set it on the table with cutlery and a roll of paper towel. 'Everything all right?'

'That was my sister, Rosa. If I'm not there she wants to know why. All the details.'

He nodded at the chopping board heaped with buttered bread. 'Did you invite them over to share?'

'Oh, shoot…' She clapped her hands to her mouth, her eyes crinkling with laughter. 'I'm used to family get-togethers.'

'It's okay, I'll make sandwiches for breakfast.'

Her phone rang again. 'Hi, Dad,' he heard her say. He

watched the humour fade, her teeth nibble on her lower lip. 'Yes, of course. I'll make sure, Dad. No, I—'

She rubbed the frown between her brows as her father obviously cut her off. Damon could hear the tirade from where he was standing, but couldn't make out the words. Just the tone. Demanding, bordering on rude.

'It's just that I thought…' She trailed off. 'Tell Mum I'm sorry. Yes. Bye.'

When she'd disconnected, he slid the fish onto plates. 'Problem?'

She seemed to be making an effort to force negative thoughts away. 'No.' She piled the buttered bread onto a plate and nodded at the meal. 'It looks good. Let's eat.'

They ate at one end of a tiny table crammed with papers. Sounds of traffic on the busy suburban road outside and other tenants coming and going filtered through the open window.

'So you have an extended family,' Damon said as they tucked into their meal.

'My mother's Italian, what do you think?'

'Your dad?'

'His mother and his father's mother were from Italy. He's a born and bred Aussie with the heart of an Italian.' She bit off a mouthful of bread and chewed on it, staring into middle space, and he got the feeling she was thinking about her phone call. 'And somewhat…inflexible. Rosa and I come from a conservative family with a bunch of conservative relatives.'

'She lives at home with your parents?'

'Only because she's getting married in a few weeks' time. She went on an overseas holiday, met this French guy… That was four months ago. Anyway, Léon's given up his job to come over here and be with her. It's all so exciting and romantic.'

He caught a glimpse of that misty gaze women got in their eyes at the mention of romance. 'You think so? Holiday romance.' He shook his head. 'I give it six months.'

Her cutlery stilled. 'You don't know either of them, yet you pronounce it dead already. You're a real cynic, you know that? I pity the woman who marries you.'

'Don't. There's not going to be one. I like my life the way it is. More wine?' He refilled their glasses of chardonnay without waiting for an answer. Conversations about marriage and commitment always made him jumpy.

'Which is how?'

'Uncomplicated. Unencumbered.'

'Irresponsible.' She downed half her wine in one hit as if she was angry—or was it envy?—and eyed him over the rim of her glass.

He shrugged. After all, that was what his parents were. But just for a moment he wondered if he'd inherited that same trait. He was a risk-taker to the point of recklessness—was that irresponsible? No. Not when he had no one to answer to.

So it suited him fine to let her think that. She didn't need to know he'd been involved in businesses in Asia and the US, had apartments in Kuala Lumpur and Phoenix. A dozen or more places where he could drop in at a moment's notice and still get a room in the best hotels in the world. She didn't need to know he could turn a profit on anything he put his mind to.

And he couldn't have done it with a wife and kids hanging off his shirt-tails.

Not that he'd planned it. Wealth per se didn't interest him. It had started as the challenge of putting what little he'd had into a failing enterprise, cranking it up, then selling at a profit. And all the while he'd been indulging other interests, taking other risks. Living in the Now. Remembering Bonita and how life didn't offer second chances and that it could all be over tomorrow.

'Bryce wanted to make you a partner in the business five years ago and you turned him down.' Her voice intruded on his thoughts.

'He knew why.' Five years ago he'd been one step ahead of his demons and up to his neck pulling a particularly challenging business he'd bought out of the red. He hadn't been ready to come back to Australia.

He took a long slow gulp of wine. 'I bet you're responsible, Kate.' He heard the almost mocking lilt in his own voice. 'Doing what people expect from you. Toeing the line. No running off to chase your dreams.'

She set her glass down with a clunk and he knew he'd hit the mark. 'Is that what you did?' she said with asperity. 'Chase your dreams no matter who you hurt or what the consequences?'

No, he'd been running away from his nightmares. 'Something like that.' Her wistful tone when she mentioned dreams had him leaning forward. 'What do you want, Kate?'

'To be the best in my chosen career.'

He shook his head. 'Nope, sounds like something your father would say. What do you really want? Deep down where it's just you.'

She was quiet for several seconds, her head resting on an upturned palm as she stared into space, her eyes mellowed with the wine she'd drunk. 'Sometimes I just want to break out of my mould, you know? Go against expectations. Be someone else, even if it's just for a little while.'

Yeah, he knew. 'You could start like this…' He reached behind her head, undid the clasp imprisoning her hair and let it flow down her back in a ripple of black satin. Watched her eyes widen, darken as he ran his fingers through its length. So soft, so silky.

'I don't wear my hair down at work. It's…it's not a professional image.'

He felt the subtle tremor run through her body at his touch. 'You're not at the office now.'

It was a simple matter to remove one gold loop earring, then the other. He massaged one lobe gently between thumb and forefinger.

His hand curved inward to curl around the back of her neck. Skin as soft and smooth as her hair. Vulnerable where her pulse fluttered wildly just above her collarbone.

His gaze dropped to her luscious coral lips. He couldn't stop himself—he soothed a finger over the seam of her mouth, remembering how he'd done exactly that on the first night he'd seen her. He traced each lip—the shape, the texture.

Kate stared at him, unable to stop him. Not wanting to stop him. She'd never seen a man look at her the way Damon Gillespie looked at her. His actions were slow, unthreatening, almost hypnotic.

'Don't you like who you are, Kate?'

*When you look at me like that I feel like the only woman in the world.*

She was sure he'd make any woman the centre of his world while it lasted, make her *feel* the centre of his universe. He'd be focused, considerate, passionate. She already knew how he made love—with single-minded intensity.

'Of course I do. But sometimes…' She must be under some sort of hypnotic trance because she wanted that same single-minded intensity driving into her again. Now. Knowing who he was: Damon Gillespie, adventurer, risk-taker. Boss.

Knowing who she was. Kate Fielding, travel agent, who never put a foot wrong.

Very unwise, but she didn't want to think about that now. For a fleeting moment she wanted to bathe in the warmth of his gaze.

'Sometimes you like to be someone else,' he said softly.

'I…' Her words trailed away as she watched him. The clarity and intensity of his gaze took away her ability to think rationally.

His finger left her lips to trace the curve of her jaw. 'Is that when Shakira comes out to play?'

She blinked. Her breath caught, her mind whirled with the erotic images. The heat of humiliation stabbed through her, hot darts stinging her face. 'No! Yes…' The way he said it, as if Shakira were a regular occurrence—did he think she slept around? Given the swiftness of their coming together, she could understand it, but she'd never played that game before. She didn't even know the rules. *'No.'*

Right now she wished she were safely tucked up in bed alone and not forced to look into those discerning eyes that saw straight through her. No, he didn't think she was easy, she decided; he thought she was a novice out for a walk on that wild side she'd managed to steer clear of. Until Saturday night.

Right now she didn't know which was worse. From somewhere deep down she felt the first prickles of resentment. He didn't know her, he didn't know how confined her life was, how restricted she felt even in her own apartment. She was still doing what her parents expected of her, for heaven's sake.

Anger was preferable and a damn sight more empowering than the impotence of embarrassment. She pulled away from his hand, which was still stroking her jaw. 'You knew. You've known all along, haven't you?'

'You didn't think I'd forget that little beauty spot?' He reached out and skimmed the place beneath her eye with a feather-light touch.

A flush rose up her neck and spread into her face—she could feel its heat as her hand rose without thought to her left cheekbone. 'Knowing and not telling me you knew is *cheating.*' The words scraped over a dry throat but pride kept her eyes on his. He'd probably been having a good laugh behind her back—boring workaholic Kate from the office.

'You knew who *I* was,' he pointed out in a reasonable tone. He smiled, his eyes warm, sharing her secret. 'Guess we're both guilty.'

She didn't *want* him sharing her secret. 'Just for the record, *Shakira* didn't exist until Saturday night,' she clipped, angry with herself for that stupidly impulsive act, angry at him for catching her out. Like a fool she'd acted a part she had no experience of and with no thought for the consequences. Wrenching her eyes from his, she pushed up, turned to grab her jacket and bag.

A firm hand gripped her arm and he swung her to face him. 'I know.'

Yep, she was that inexperienced. She was so out of her depth with a man like Damon. 'I don't think—' She glimpsed the flash of challenge in his eyes before his mouth crashed down on hers, hot and urgent and demanding.

Stars burst. Worlds collided. She'd never been kissed like this—with passion, and something more. Something deeper. Her lips burned and her toes curled as the lightning sensation jagged through her body. As his hands moulded around her bottom and purposely pulled her flush against his granite-hard erection.

She fought back a moan that sprang from deep inside. She was losing control and she couldn't afford to let him see. Not now. Not till they'd talked—later. When she *was* in control. Tugging at her bag, she tried to jerk away.

Immediately he lifted his head, loosened his hold on her buttocks. His eyes still gleamed with that spark of challenge. 'Think about that, Kate.'

'I…I have to go.' She dragged in air. 'Leave. Me. Alone.'

He stepped back, giving her space. 'You need a lift.'

She tightened her fingers around the strap of her bag so he wouldn't see how they trembled. 'No. There's a taxi stand outside.'

She moved to the door and pulled it open. Traffic whizzed by as a cold breeze whipped through her silk blouse, chilling her flesh. He kept pace with her, his bare feet slapping on the wet concrete as she hurried down the few steps to the pavement.

She spotted a cab—thank goodness—and ran towards it, waving a hand. The cab pulled to the kerb and the instant it stopped she pulled the door open, then turned to him. 'Thank you for dinner.'

His hands in his pockets, his stance was casual but his eyes signalled something else entirely. 'I want to see you again.'

For a moment her heart beat hard in her chest, but was it really Kate he wanted to see, or was it as straight forward as easy sex? Like Nick. She slid onto the seat with a mirthless laugh. 'Oh, I'm sure you will.' She was his employee after all, however hotly she denied it to his face.

'*Outside* of office hours,' he said as he closed the cab door.

She looked away as the cab pulled into the traffic. That kiss was something to think about all right, she thought, out of breath as she sank back onto the seat. If she wanted, there could be a lot more. *After* they'd talked.

But whatever happened, it was temporary, she reminded herself. She'd been hurt before when the man she'd thought she loved—the man she'd thought loved her—walked away with another woman. But this wasn't love, this was lust. A simple attraction and she knew up front it wasn't going anywhere with a man like Damon. Would she allow herself the pleasure of being up close with him again before he left the country and moved on to wherever the fancy took him next?

# CHAPTER SIX

Six a.m. Damon rubbed a hand over gritty eyes as he glanced at the clock in Bry's office and rotated his shoulders to ease the stiffness. Two and a half hours before staff arrived. Too much to do, no time to go home and change. He already knew if he didn't do something quickly to correct the downward spiral, Aussie Essential Travel was headed for bad times even sooner than he'd expected.

Kate had left him with no alternative but to go to bed alone and, after a couple of hours of restless frustration, he'd given up on sleep and driven to the agency. What he'd confirmed had consigned his hopes for a quick sale to the sewer.

According to Kate, Bry had managed the accounting side of his business, and his uncle was no accountant. He stretched out the kinks some more while he stared at the evidence on the computer screen.

Then he settled down, tapped a few more keys and prepared to transfer some of his US funds to his account in Australia. This time the business would succeed, he'd make sure of it. He felt a stir of enthusiasm. It was yet another challenge, and he loved nothing more, be it an ailing business or an unfamiliar BASE jump.

Or one irresistibly sexy woman.

Kate. He'd almost had her last night. He couldn't remember a time when he'd wanted a woman more than he'd wanted Kate. Her unique fragrance seemed to be permanently lodged in his nostrils, the imprint of her lips indelibly etched on his.

She'd been all but putty in his hands until he'd mentioned Shakira. It wasn't a big deal, a bit of fun—they both admitted they'd avoided mentioning it—but she'd turned from malleable to rigid in two seconds flat.

That didn't deter him. He wasn't finished with Kate Fielding by a long shot. Damon slurped the remainder of black coffee that had turned cold two hours ago as he opened a new file on Bry's computer and got to work. Before he left Australia he intended having this business on the road to recovery.

He also intended having Kate in his bed before he was done.

Since she'd tossed and turned all night with images of Damon intruding into her dreams, Kate woke feeling edgy and irritable. Only a coward would leave an issue unresolved the way she had last night. So he'd cheated about his knowledge of Shakira—she had to admit they'd both cheated.

She dumped home-made muesli into a bowl and added milk. Her parents would have a major fit if they knew what their oldest daughter had done. She'd always been the sensible one. While Rosa had always done her own thing, the ever dutiful Katerina had tried to please. And who was the golden girl now? Not Kate.

While she waited for her English Breakfast tea bag to steep, she paced the kitchen. It wasn't her fault Nick had walked out on their relationship, although her mother hadn't seen it that way. Like Nick Angelos, Mum had fully expected her to give up her career, make a home and fill it with *molti bambini Italiani*. After all, she'd been twenty-six, past time to settle down and provide her with grandchildren.

What she'd never told her mother was that while her coworker/lover Nick and Kate had been sharing a room on an educational tour of the Maldives, he'd been sharing a little more—a lot more—of himself with another Aussie travel agent three rooms away.

Let Rosa have the honour of giving her the first grandkid— a French-Italian Aussie. Grabbing her mug of tea, she carried it to the table. She was moving on with her own life goals. *Career* goals. First up, her promised promotion—she intended holding Damon to it.

Next she was going to come clean with him about that crazy *one-off* night. She wanted to make doubly sure he knew she did *not* do one-night stands, that she'd never set out to seduce or be seduced by anyone. Ever.

She shook her head, then plopped onto a kitchen chair. Did it matter what he thought? Last night had demonstrated there was something more between them than just sex. Or had it? Was that just her romantic side, a slightly desperate woman's wishful thinking? She'd always held to the idea that she could have a relationship and her career, but it hadn't worked out that way. Which left her with the career option.

How did *he* feel? She'd seen so much in his eyes, but, again, was it because she saw what she wanted to see? He'd kissed her with demanding passion and skill, made damn sure she knew what he wanted. Physically.

So that would be enough, she told herself. She would keep any emotions right out of it, the way he did. He wasn't going to be here long; physical was all she wanted from him. Short-term sex and the promise of that promotion before he sold the business to someone else.

When she stepped into the office at ten past eight she was already in a spin in anticipation of seeing Damon. She knew he was already there because she'd seen his car in the car park and felt a moment's pique that he'd arrived before her. He'd mentioned something about coming in today to work in Bryce's office and was obviously a morning person.

Sandy, too, was already at her desk, but jumped up with a smile as Kate entered. 'Hi, Kate.'

'Hi.' Kate wondered what the somewhat breathlessness in Sandy's greeting meant as she hooked her umbrella on the cloak stand. Or could she guess—Damon had already charmed her with his presence this morning? Another emotion slid through her as she took in Sandy's rapt expression, making her feel positively queasy.

Sandy rounded her desk and sidled up to Kate, fanning a hand in front of her face. 'Well, well, well.'

'Excuse me?'

'A little office romance, Kate?'

'Who?' Kate said, straightening her suit jacket and feigning ignorance. But her pulse was already one guilty step ahead of her.

'You and Damon Gillespie.' She darted ahead of Kate, hitched herself on the edge of Kate's desk, her straight skirt riding up her thighs. 'And here I was thinking you couldn't stand the man.' She leaned forward with a conspiratorial grin. 'Tell me all.'

Kate smoothed damp palms down the front of her own skirt and forced herself to walk unhurriedly to her desk. 'There's nothing to tell. We inspected a few agencies in the area.' Then, in case Damon had already mentioned it, she said, 'Followed by a bite to eat.'

'A bite.' Sandy smirked and Kate wondered if Damon had left a mark on her neck at some stage and tried to swallow over a dry throat.

'Yes.'

'Are you sure you're not leaving out a teensy tiny detail?'

'No,' she stated emphatically. 'Even if what you're implying were true, *which it's not*, it couldn't be an office romance because he *doesn't work here*…' She trailed off as she came around to the front of her desk. There was a staff memo printed under the office logo requesting she attend an eight-thirty staff meeting. Personally signed by Damon Gillespie.

On top she saw her gold earrings attached with sticky tape to a neon-green note with the damning words, 'You forgot these last night. D.' Obviously Sandy had been busy this morning. Minding other people's business.

'It's not what you think,' she began, snatching up the offending jewellery and crushing the incriminating note in her fist as heat rushed to her cheeks.

'And who the hell does he think he is, demanding a staff meeting?' she rushed on, fired up now and ready to detonate something or someone, and Damon was top of her list. 'He's not a member of our team, and, besides, he's not staying.' The staff meeting was *her* job—it had been her job for years—and she already had an agenda ready to roll. 'Where's Bill? And Maureen doesn't start till ten—'

'Morning, Kate.' The sound of Damon's voice behind her made her jump as if she'd been caught dipping her hand in the till. 'I've notified everyone,' he informed her. 'They'll all be here.'

She closed her eyes a moment to pull herself together, then opened them very quickly when she felt firm hands squeeze her shoulders once. 'Don't stress, Miz Fielding, it's all under control.'

All under *his* control. Annoyance prickled along her skin. She refrained from the immediate urge to shake him off, since the action would only make *her* look like the bad guy and give the wide-eyed Sandy even more to gossip about. She didn't want his hands on her, it made her remember, muddled her thoughts and she wanted to stay *mad*. If she was angry at least it gave her the feeling that she was in control.

Bill and Maureen arrived at the same time with a chorus of, 'Good morning, Damon.'

'Good morning, all. If you want to grab a coffee first, we'll get started.'

Inside, Kate steamed at his presumption, but she forced a cardboard smile at the staff as a couple headed for the small kitchenette and Damon's Big Coffee Machine while the others walked to the meeting room.

Since he was behind her, she didn't turn and look at him until she'd collected her composure along with her notepad and pen and by then he was already walking towards the staffroom. She might be humming with indignation, but her stupid pulse jittered at the sight of his broad shoulders filling the short corridor and the way the black jersey stretched tight across his back... She gaped at the sight.

Black T-shirt and those jungle-green cargo pants—the ones he'd worn Saturday night. For a staff meeting! What had happened to the expensive suit he'd worn on Monday? It must have been a fluke—obviously he had no idea about appropriate dress code. Or he didn't give a damn.

She compressed her lips into a hard line as she followed, *not* noticing his masculine scent wafting behind him. *Not* seeing the glint of auburn in his hair as he passed beneath the corridor's fluorescent light, nor the sexy strip of tanned neck that tempted her beyond reason.

She wanted to pull him aside and tell him a lot of things, starting with how he so wasn't qualified to conduct this meeting. How he shouldn't be wearing those unsuitable pants—even if his butt did fill them out to perfection. Heat washed through her as she remembered the rough texture against her palms. Against her inner thighs...

*Back on track, Kate.* Like why he'd left her earrings on her desk for all to see—earrings *he'd* taken off—with that ambiguous note. Had he even given a thought as to how it could be interpreted? She'd be the latest office's hot gossip, if she wasn't already.

She sucked in a breath and gritted her teeth. But she

couldn't say any of those things because the rest of the staff were already filing into the room.

Damon stood behind the seat at the head of the rectangular table where he'd already placed a stack of paperwork and set up for a PowerPoint presentation. For the first time now, she met his eyes as he turned to her indicating she take the seat to his right. She saw the fleeting spark of heat, quickly banked as others took their places around the table.

'I may need some assistance,' he said, all business.

He hadn't even bothered to shave, she noticed. The dark stubble made him look even more disreputable. 'By all means, let me assist you.' *When you fall in a heap.*

He nodded at the two mugs steaming next to his paperwork. 'I got you a coffee, thought you might need it.'

'Thanks, but I prefer tea first thing in the morning.'

His smile didn't falter, but one eyebrow lifted ever so slightly and his eyes darkened as if he was suggesting they might share a more intimate 'first thing in the morning' at some point. An instant traitorous heat seared her belly.

'I'll try to remember,' he said softly.

She didn't return his smile, skirting stiffly behind him to take the requested seat at his right. If he'd just asked her for assistance in the first place, as he'd mentioned the other night, instead of trying to be the big chief, she'd have been more than happy to help. They could have worked on this together. As colleagues of course. Obviously Damon worked alone. He'd merely suggested the assistance because she'd made her antagonism clear. Condescending jerk.

He sat, spreading his hands on the table in front of him. 'Good morning, again, and welcome everyone. Thanks for coming in early at such short notice.' He glanced around the table, acknowledging each member of staff. 'First up, I'd like to thank you for your support in my absence over the past couple of weeks. It's much appreciated.'

He let the silence draw out a moment before continuing.

'As you all know, for better or worse, Aussie Essential Travel has been passed to me through Bryce's will. And I've decided not to sell at this point in time.'

Kate let that sink in. Damon was now officially her boss. She had the hots for her *boss*.

'I'm looking forward to the challenge,' he went on, 'and hoping we can pull together as a team.'

'It's great to have you on board, Damon,' Kate heard Sandy say. Others contributed similar words of welcome.

Kate stared at him, pressing her lips together to halt the words that sprang to *her* lips. Like what did he know about the travel industry? About running a business? Just because he'd seen the figures, didn't mean he knew what he was doing. Except she'd also seen the figures and agreed…

He must have read her thoughts, because he looked directly at her as he said, 'I come with a background in business. I have an executive MBA, which I gained in Australia, and have been involved in several successful business ventures both here and overseas.' His eyes twinkled as he watched her digest the information.

She sat back in her chair. She wanted to hit him. He'd given her an altogether different impression. Deliberately? 'Excuse me, but does that include the travel industry?'

His smiling eyes didn't dim. 'I have some background knowledge; perhaps you can help me fill in the gaps as we go along.'

'Didn't you say you'd only be in Australia temporarily?'

'I won't leave until I'm sure the business is running smoothly, Kate,' he assured her. 'At which time I'll appoint a manager.'

She gritted her teeth. She'd told him Bryce's plans, but he didn't give any hint that she might be considered for the position. Didn't even look in her direction as he said it. Instead he distributed a handout to go with the presentation he'd prepared and talked about recent low sales figures, their dwindling customer base and his vision for the business for the next six months.

Not the company's vision, she noted. His. She doodled on the pages and half listened to a list of improvements he proposed—something about improved advertising and special deals—and tried not to let the resentment fester inside her.

'We're changing our name and image,' he said, catching Kate's attention. 'From now on we're the Ultimate Journey Travel Agency. It's not only the destination we're selling, but the whole experience,' he explained, and clicked to the next slide; adventurers enjoying white-water rafting somewhere in New Zealand and the slogan, 'WE try before YOU buy'. 'In other words, we're selling our personal expertise. Our agency isn't picking up younger customers because we're not promoting more of the action holidays available for the twenty to thirty-fives.

'To address this, each staff member will undertake an educational in the next six months. You're all under forty, I want you to step out of your comfort zone and go somewhere new, try something you've never tried before.'

'Damon, I have young kids,' Maureen interjected. 'I can't up and leave them at this time.'

'That's fine, Maureen, we'll find something for you locally. Ever tried skydiving? Caving?'

'Uh…no…' She sank back in her chair.

Bill had no such hesitation. 'I'll give it a go,' he said with a grin.

Damon nodded. 'That's what I'm talking about. Enthusiasm. Experience.' He tapped his pen on the table. 'Kate, you're going to get the ball rolling.'

Her eyes snapped to his and were immediately held prisoner. Oh, no. She'd told him she was looking for something a little more adventurous, but she hadn't meant *adventurous* adventurous. More along the lines of experiencing something like… snow-skiing in Dubai or an Alaskan cruise.

'Bryce had an educational to Bali booked. Do you know anything about that?'

'No.'

'Well, I hope your passport's up to date.'

'Yes, it is.' She released her pent-up breath slowly. Bali sounded safe. Plenty of sand, shopping and luxury hotels, a massage or two, a cultural show. She could do Bali, no problem.

'Tuesday, then.'

Uh. 'So soon?'

'The accommodation's booked. No sense in deferring it.'

Kate nodded. She really needed to get away and the sooner, the better. Damon Gillespie was seriously bad for her health. And working with him was going to be almost impossible. She sighed inwardly. Maybe she should take that other job the agency in the next suburb had offered a couple of months ago. Nice and safe and Damon-free. Except she'd been here before him…

'That's all for now, folks.' Damon checked his watch and clicked off the computer. 'It's almost nine; time to open up. Anything you want to discuss; I'll be in Bryce's office. Kate, you'll want to see me about the details of your trip some time today.'

Damon worked solidly for the next three hours. He didn't go near Kate. But it was damn hard knowing she was only a few steps away. He knew she was busy with customers and work that had accumulated over the past couple of weeks, but that wasn't what stopped him. She was steamed up at learning he was now officially her employer and wasn't going anywhere any time soon. He'd give her time to cool off while he made some reservations himself.

He tapped his pen on the desk and stared at the wall in front of him. The devil of it was, he wanted Kate Fielding beyond what he considered reasonable. She wasn't like any other woman he'd ever dated, if 'date' was the right word—he rarely saw a woman for more than a couple of weeks, a couple of months at the most.

And those women wanted the same as him. A good time

for as long as it lasted or until either of them moved on. Temporary. No sense in becoming attached. Too many other things to do in life to hitch yourself to one person, to fall for someone who might be gone tomorrow.

Yep, everything could end tomorrow.

Kate wasn't that kind of woman. She needed the familiarity of family. The steady job, a stable environment. Listening to her last night had warned him that she wasn't his type. But Kate had dreams and was afraid to chase them. He had a feeling the only time she'd ever reached for her stars was the night she'd disguised herself as Shakira, and she'd been caught out. Damn pity for her, he thought, because she might never have the courage to try something like that again.

He glanced at his watch and realised he'd been staring into space for twenty minutes. His hand rasped over his stubble. He'd been in this office for over ten hours and was running on only two hours' sleep. He needed a jog to uncramp his muscles and get some fresh air into his lungs.

Kate clicked off the program she'd been working on and reached for her bag as Damon walked out of Bryce's office. For once he didn't look ready for action. He looked tired, his skin paler than usual beneath the stubble shadow. Almost vulnerable. Which was ridiculous.

Everything she'd learned about Damon in the past few days pointed to a man who could tackle anything or anyone. Wreak havoc if he was so inclined and leave disaster in his wake. She had the first-hand experience to prove it.

He stopped at her desk, giving her an up-close view of the fatigue bruises beneath his eyes. 'Going somewhere?' he said.

'I was just going to grab some lunch—at the coffee place. Across the road.' *Next door to the pub where we had sex on Saturday night.* Then because she felt some inexplicable obligation as a fellow worker, she asked, 'Can I get you something?'

'Thanks, but I'll come with you. We can talk while we eat.'

From the corner of her eye she saw Sandy watching them and immediately backed away. 'Um…I was going to eat at my desk.'

'No,' he said firmly. 'You've been at it all morning, you need a break and so do I.' He placed a hand in the centre of her back, the other he raised to Sandy. 'Back in half an hour.'

'What's the problem?' he said when they stepped outside. 'If you avoid me like the plague people'll think I have BO or something.' He lifted his arm and sniffed. 'I don't, do I?'

When she didn't reply, he said, 'I've been here since two a.m., perhaps I have and you're too polite to tell me.'

She looked at him in astonishment. 'Two a.m.? Why?'

He slowed, watching her. 'Why do you think, Kate?'

The memory of last night's kiss slow-burned in his eyes. The heat swirling between them as he'd plastered his lips to hers. How he'd pressed his erection against her, making her ache for more than just a kiss.

She dragged her gaze away before she did or said something foolish, like, *Why didn't you come over to my place, and we could have been sleepless together,* and kept walking.

They covered the remaining few metres to the coffee shop in silence, purchased sandwiches and coffee and sat at one of the little tables.

Kate struggled with the cling wrap around her sandwich. 'You left my earrings and that damn note out for the world to see.'

His brow puckered. 'Uh. I never gave it a thought. Is that a problem for you?'

'Did you even think about what you wrote: *you forgot these last night?* Sandy's the world's biggest gossip.' She stirred her coffee with a vengeance. 'I don't do office romance.'

His hand hovered over his latte and interest sparked in his eyes as they met hers. 'Is that what we have, Kate?'

'What… Romance?'

She almost scoffed. As if he'd do romance. He'd simply

*do*. A shiver ran down her spine but her face flushed with heat at the memory. He'd already proved he could *do* masterfully well. She frowned into her cappuccino. He was undeniably her boss now. Damn.

'If that's what you want to call it,' he said softly.

'I don't know what I call it,' she said, irritation pricking her skin. 'All I know is I can't damn well get you out of my head.'

She didn't realise she'd admitted it aloud, but she must have because he said, 'Me, too.' He leaned closer, touched her hand with one long bronzed finger. 'And I want to take it further, see where it leads. So I'm coming to Bali with you.'

# CHAPTER SEVEN

'YOU'RE coming too?' Kate stared at Damon, her coffee forgotten. Everything forgotten.

'Hopefully,' he said, amusement twinkling in his eyes and she got that he wasn't referring to accompanying her, but something far more intimate.

Heat swirled through her, and her cheeks burned. He'd also voiced several disturbing suggestions at the staff meeting. Like stepping out of one's comfort zone. Trying new things. Scary things. 'That's…not a good idea.'

'Why not?'

'Because…you and I have very different ideas about what a holiday is.'

'Ah, Kate, you're forgetting; this isn't a vacation, it's an *educational*.'

'Which makes it blazingly obvious you're my boss now. How will the other staff view it? Us?'

'As far as they're concerned it's strictly business. What we do in our own time, after business hours, is no one else's concern. Kate…' He stroked her hand again, then lifted and rotated it so that his palm rubbed against hers. His eyes darkened; his smile sobered. 'I told you I want to see you again. I'm attracted to you. I was attracted to you from the moment I first laid eyes on you.'

'You were attracted to a veiled belly-dancer; the unknown

appealed to you. You saw me as a challenge or a mystery parcel to unwrap.'

'And you were attracted to Indiana Jones. Kate Fielding would never have sex with a bad-to-the-bone stranger. Kate's never even had one-night sex, has she.' A statement, not a question.

Another wave of heat rushed to her face. He made it sound like a character flaw. 'That's none of your business.'

He tightened his hand when she would have pulled it away. 'A word of advice: if you want to be Shakira, go to a crowded nightclub, preferably on the other side of town. Don't do it surrounded by people you know; worse still, your colleagues. You're bound to be caught out.'

As she had been. She tugged her hand again, and this time she broke free. Mortified. She was mortified. She felt as if he'd stripped her naked to the bare bones. 'Thank you so much for your words of wisdom. If you'll excuse me, poor sex-deprived *Kate Fielding* has work to do.' She pushed up and out of her chair.

'For goodness' sake, Kate, sit down.' He caught her arm before she could pass him, the challenge in his eyes breaking down her defences as fast as she built them. 'Don't you know how much of a turn-on it was to know you wanted me when it was clearly something you didn't normally do?'

'Will you stop grabbing at me and holding me against my will?'

'It's not against your will.' He released her arm to prove it.

Kate was tempted to march off just to prove a point, but something kept her standing there with the scent of his testosterone temptingly close. 'How did you know? About…the no sex…' She tilted her chin and looked down at him at the same time. 'So I can rectify it the next time…I see someone I fancy.'

His eyes narrowed. 'In that case I'm not going to tell you. Sit.'

She did as he asked only because her legs were wobbly,

scooped her half-finished coffee towards her and drank the remainder in a couple of deep gulps to moisten her throat. This whole situation was surreal. 'Why would you want me when you know who I am now and you're clearly attracted to another type of woman?'

His eyes dropped to her breasts, hidden beneath her suit jacket. Just as well, too, since her nipples immediately puckered against her bra.

'Why don't we explore that notion?' he said after a pause.

The idea of exploring took flight in Kate's imagination, making a mockery of her earlier determination to avoid office complications. *Why don't we?*

Sensing her warming to the idea, he continued, 'Let's take this opportunity to get to know one another better, for however long we've got.'

*In other words: temporary.* More, 'You make it sound terminal.' But at least she knew where she stood.

'We won't know if we don't give it a go. The holiday of a lifetime.'

'*Educational,*' she corrected. 'Whatever you call it, I'm not camping out and I'm not skydiving or bungee jumping or doing any of those…' she waved a hand '…dangerous things.' Of which letting Damon accompany her to Bali was one.

'Where's your sense of adventure?'

'In permanent hibernation.'

'I promise we won't camp out. Or bungee jump.'

He grinned, making his stubbled cheeks crease in an alarming way. It did serious things to her internal organs. It made her want to reach out and run a finger down the groove beside his mouth. She tightened her fingers around her empty cup. 'That's two. What about the rest?'

He leaned back, his eyes still sparkling. 'We're travelling first class. Score one for you. Two—the hotel's only recently opened—five-star luxury. I'll make you a deal. I choose the daytime activities, you choose what we do nights.'

*Nights*. Her choice. In other words he was giving her the option of whether or not they had sex. The truth was she'd have preferred it the other way round. She had a feeling they'd both agree on what they wanted to do in the evening. At midnight. Before dawn.

But in daylight hours...' What sort of activities?'

'Ever been paragliding?'

Images of being suspended in a harness with nothing between her and certain death flashed through her mind before the image morphed into what she'd spent years trying to forget. Pain stabbed through her heart but no way would she allow him to see. She shook it away. 'No, and I don't intend to.'

'Ridden a motorbike?'

Big Harley-Davidson. Just her and jungle boy and a big throbbing machine between her legs... She might be tempted.

'Say yes, Kate. I'll even go to one of those cultural shows with you if you're interested in that kind of thing.'

'What am I saying yes to—you accompanying me or your so-called deal?'

'I'm going with you, that's a definite, but the deal's a suggestion.'

She mulled over his *suggestion*. It sounded more like a dare. A dare she couldn't accept. Could she?

Damon studied her while he finished his sandwich. He'd thrown the idea out as a challenge. When she'd threatened to walk out on him, he'd felt the beginnings of something like panic, which of course it wasn't—but there'd been an uncomfortable clench in his gut, the kind he'd felt when he'd taken his first jump. Suddenly there'd been only one thing on his mind. Kate. All of Kate.

He shouldn't have taunted her about Shakira. He was feeling good about the fact that she'd told him she didn't sleep around. That she'd made an exception for him.

'Luxury and adventure,' she mused aloud.

'You got it.' Kate wasn't much of a risk-taker, he was discovering, but he wanted her to be, for her own self-esteem if nothing else, and he had a feeling she wasn't going to let him see her back down. In fact, he was counting on it.

'Why not?' she agreed.

He leaned back. 'My sentiments exactly. You only live once.' But there was something in her dark-eyed gaze that niggled at him as he spoke the words.

Damon didn't see much of Kate on her own over the next few days. In the office she was all business and obviously didn't want to be seen to be too cosy with the boss. Which was okay since he was bogged down with the mess Bryce had left behind in addition to his own Internet business, which was currently taking a back seat.

She went home on Friday night before he realised and when he left the office and rolled into bed at one a.m. it was too late to call. He spent the entire weekend at the office, knowing he'd be away the following week.

On Sunday evening he phoned her. The sound of her 'Kate Fielding' on the other end of the phone was a bright spark in a hard day's night.

'Hello, Kate. You packed yet?'

'Damon.'

Rolling his chair away from the desk, he closed his eyes and leaned back. He loved the way she said his name in that almost proper but smoky velvet way that caressed his senses. It made him want to drive right over to her apartment and hear it up close and personal. Close enough for her to murmur it against his ear. Better still, to hear her moan it. Against his mouth, over his chest, his—

'Hi, and no. I still have tomorrow. Didn't you say I could take tomorrow to get organised?' All business now.

He swiped a hand over his eyes and grinned, imagining her behind his closed eyelids, curled up on her sofa, her hair down around her shoulders, damp and fragrant with shampoo. 'This from the girl who never takes time off.'

There was a pause and he could hear her elevated breathing. 'You make me do crazy things.'

He hoped. He sincerely hoped—he had a lot of ideas for those ten days. 'It's not crazy to take a day off to prepare for a demanding and strenuous business trip.'

'Not too strenuous. You promised. And I think the word "luxury" was mentioned somewhere.'

'So it was.' He smiled again, remembering the spa baths mentioned on the hotel's website. No doubt she'd need it after some of the activities he had in mind, both in and out of the bedroom. 'What are you doing?'

'Now? I'm researching Bali on my laptop. In bed.'

Had she purposely slipped that little tidbit of information in? 'And what have you uncovered?' No—*discovered*. Damon had meant discovered.

'That some beaches have white sand and some have black. I'm watching a video clip…brilliant blue water and black sand.'

'We'll find it and take a swim there.'

They talked for a few more moments about details of the trip and arrangements he'd set in place for staff to cover for them while they were away.

'I'll see you Tuesday morning, then,' he said. 'The taxi will pick us up from your place at ten a.m. Don't forget to pack a swimsuit.'

He thumbed the disconnect button and remained with eyes closed a moment more. He hadn't had a woman's company in a while and now he was going to be with one very appealing Kate Fielding 24/7 for over a week.

How would that work? He couldn't wait to find out.


'So why haven't we met this new boss of yours?' Kate's father said when she rang to say goodbye on Monday evening. She wished Rosa had answered the call.

'It's not like we're dating, Dad. You don't bring your boss home for tea.' Not even when you've had wild sex. Especially not when you've had wild sex.

'Didn't stop you from eating tea at his house the other night.'

'I'm sorry I cancelled at the last minute, but Damon was alone. He asked me to stay; I couldn't say no. We had work to do,' she remembered to say at the last moment.

'I hope you don't go along with everything he asks of you outside office hours, Katerina. You need to stand up for yourself.'

Kate felt the familiar prickle of annoyance. She *needed* to stand up to her *father*. 'I *wanted* to stay, okay? The work doesn't go away because you ignore it.'

'The least you could have done was invite him over here instead so we could meet him. You're going overseas with this man alone—you know how your mother is.'

*Not so much Mum as you, Dad.* '*Work*, Dad. We're going to be working the whole time,' she lied. 'It's not a holiday. And I'm old enough to take care of myself,' she added, as if it would make a difference. Sometimes she Just Wanted To Scream.

'If you'd married Nick you wouldn't have to go out to work.'

*There it was*—the unspoken message that she'd have produced a baby or two by now. She closed her eyes and pinched the bridge of her nose. '*Nick* left *me*, remember?' Because she'd wanted to have a career as well as a marriage. Because he'd betrayed her with another woman who was prepared to give up her own life to keep house and have his babies.

'I'll ring when I get there,' she said before she disconnected. The usual routine when she went overseas—ring home daily or expect management to chase all over the hotel for her with messages from home.

She breathed a sigh of relief, then immediately drew in

one of anticipation laced with bat wings that lurched crazily in her stomach. This time tomorrow night she'd be in Bali. With Damon.

'You're not wearing a business suit all the way to Bali.' Damon winced inwardly as he took in the very properly suited Kate standing at her front door, her glorious black hair clipped back in a severe knot. The only redeeming factor was the pencil-slim skirt that finished a good three inches above her knees.

'I always travel in business attire on an educational.' She cast a censorious glance at his jeans and T-shirt as she spoke.

'Not this time.'

All along he'd told Kate that was what they were doing, but he realised now he'd conjured up an entirely different scenario. He'd not been certain she'd go along with him if she'd known that the whole *educational* concept he'd initiated was to get closer to her. 'Go change, we have plenty of time. And if there are any more suits of armour in your luggage, take them out.'

She seemed to think about it for a long time, as if weighing up her answer, then said, 'No.'

He bit back on his surprise. 'Kate. You won't be comfortable flying across the country in that.'

She shook her head. 'I'm well acquainted with flying across countries in a business suit. You might be my boss, but you can't tell me how to dress out of office hours. It's you who should be changing. What does your dress code say about you? About the business you represent?'

He watched defiance flash in her dark eyes. Better, he thought with approval, than what he'd heard when she'd spoken to her father; she needed to cultivate more of it. 'What if I told you it wasn't strictly an educational?'

Apart from the merest flicker, her expression didn't alter. As if she'd known all along. 'Doesn't make a speck of difference. The suit stays.'

Her gaze remained fused with his, the tacit mutual acknowledgement of what they were about to embark on shimmering like a heat haze between them.

His skin prickled with that same heat as it spread to other parts of his body. He stepped nearer. 'At least let your hair down.' Without waiting for the refusal he reached behind her head and removed the tortoiseshell clip. The thick ebony length cascaded around her face, and he tunnelled his fingers into its silken fragrance as he drew it over her shoulders.

'Oh.' She spun the words out with devastatingly obvious effect. 'I fully intend to do just that.'

Her coral lips pouted up at him, tantalisingly plump, temptingly close. 'Then let's get started,' he murmured, and, taking her at her word, he bent his head and slid his mouth over hers.

There was no hint of surrender in her kiss as she leaned into him. Just the smooth caramel taste of Kate. He dipped his tongue between her lips to savour the taste more deeply, lingered a moment before straightening and meeting her eyes with shared anticipation.

It was going to be an 'educational' after all, he mused, albeit not the sort he'd mapped out for the staff at last week's meeting. He was looking forward to learning all there was to know about Kate Fielding.

They arrived at Denpasar International Airport mid-evening. The heavy humidity hit Kate like a physical wall as they exited into the tropical evening air, making her feel clammy and queasy as Damon ushered her into the air-conditioned hotel limousine hired to collect them. It had been all she could do to stand upright as they went through customs and immigration.

'You okay?' Damon studied her as they settled onto the plush leather seats.

'A little tired. It's nearly midnight Sydney time. I'm usually tucked up in bed before now.'

At her mention of bedtime the air thickened. After that devastating kiss on her doorstep before they left Kate knew exactly what Damon's intentions were for this trip—and he knew hers. Earlier in the afternoon she'd been beside herself with anticipation, but right now her mind wasn't on anything except sleep. It was becoming impossible to ignore the nausea that had plagued her for the last couple of hours of the flight. But the flight hadn't been excessively turbulent and the business-class cabin had been a welcome change from the cramped economy class she usually travelled in.

Fifteen minutes later they arrived at Nusa Dua beach and their hotel lobby came into view. The limo slowed to a stop. For a moment she forgot her discomfort as they made their way towards the check-in desk. Huge white columns surrounded by potted palms supported the lobby's vaulted teak ceiling. Overhead fans stirred the air. A tranquil pool surrounded by a variety of bougainvillea reflected a purple silk sky and a pearlescent moon.

But a sudden cramp knifed through her belly, catching her mid-stride. The sticky sensation of sweat trickling down her back under her blouse and the pungent smell of tropical fruit on the heavy air made her feel faint. She pressed her dry lips together. She'd been in the tropics before and it had never affected her like this.

Thankfully Damon's attention was elsewhere as he spoke to the exotic Balinese woman behind the desk in traditional dress. Kate dragged herself over to his side.

'*Selamat datang*, Mr Gillespie, Mrs Gillespie. Welcome.' The woman, whose name tag said Mari, smiled graciously at them. 'Your suite is ready for you. Enjoy your stay.'

Kate's head reeled. *Mrs Gillespie?*

'There's been a mistake,' she heard Damon say as if he were speaking from the other side of the lobby. 'We didn't book a suite.'

'You are Mr Gillespie, *ya*?'

'*Ya.*'

Mari rechecked her computer. 'You have booked a suite.' She looked at Damon, then Kate, her brow creased. 'You are not married?'

'No.' Damon's voice sounded as hard and unyielding as the marble tiles beneath Kate's feet.

She heard him speak her name, but a swarm of insects buzzed in her ears and Damon transformed into a shimmering figure that seemed to fade in and out like a bad black and white TV reception.

She licked chalk-dry lips. 'I…' Then the screen went black.

Damon caught her as she crumpled, hauling her limp body up against him. She was as white as the marble floor, her thick lashes against her high cheekbones. And out cold.

'She is not used to the weather here,' Mari said over his shoulder.

'Maybe.' He hoped that was all it was. With an arm beneath her legs, he swept her into his arms. 'Forget changing our reservation, just show me the way.'

He followed a worried Mari to the nearest lift and down a corridor. The door at the end swung open as he carried her in, laid her on the huge king-size bed, barely noticing the luxury décor, the flower and fruit arrangement. The bottle of champagne cooling in the bucket.

'I will call the doctor,' Mari said, hovering at his side.

'Thank you, but we'll give her a moment.' He sat down beside her and saw her eyelids flicker. 'No need for you to stay. I'll ring down if anything changes.'

His eyes didn't leave Kate as Mari left, switching on the overhead fan on her way out. He pushed the perspiration-damp hair off Kate's brow. 'Kate?'

A soft knock at the door drew him away from the bed a moment. The porter delivered their bags, glanced at the bed and left quickly. Damon resumed his place beside her and kept watch.

The eyelids flickered and opened. Dark eyes stared up at

him like deep pools against her whiter than white complexion. She pushed up quickly. 'I...need...bathroom,' she muttered urgently, her hand over her mouth. 'Now!'

He glanced around. 'This way.' He swung her off the bed, carried her to the nearest door, pushed it open and set her down.

'Go away,' she said, slamming the door in his face.

The uncomfortably explicit sounds on the other side had him walking quickly away to give her privacy, grabbing the room's cordless phone on his way. He slid open the slatted doors that led to their private balcony and strode into the balmy evening and a moonlit panorama of tranquillity.

He rang through to Reception. 'I requested *adjoining* rooms,' he told the apologetic man on the other end, and was informed the original booking had been for a suite. This evening there were no vacant rooms and the problem would be sorted out tomorrow. If Mr Gillespie so desired, a maid could be sent to prepare the couch in the lounge area.

'That won't be necessary,' Damon said, and disconnected. He wouldn't get a moment's sleep anyway until he knew Kate was okay. He glanced at the closed bathroom door, wondering if he should check on her, but then he heard her swear in a way he'd never have expected and the sound of water running. She was conscious at least.

He toed off his shoes, walked out onto the cool sand a few steps from their balcony and stared at the ripples on the water. One thing he could almost guarantee: Kate wouldn't take kindly to this arrangement, regardless of what was developing between them. Bryce had made the original reservation, so the name Gillespie would remain the same. His uncle had booked a suite. Damon shook his head. The man had had champagne tastes and a cheap beer income. Who knew why he'd even booked the trip? Damon doubted it was an educational.

Would Kate believe the mix-up was exactly that? How would it affect the rest of their stay? He blew out a breath. He'd know soon enough.

# CHAPTER EIGHT

WHEN Damon stepped back inside fifteen minutes later, Kate was fast asleep. The moon's silver beams shone through the door's slats to caress her body. But her skirt was twisted around her thighs, her blouse looked as if it was strangling her. Even with the moving air beneath the fan, perspiration sheened her face and neck.

He couldn't leave her to sleep like that. He shook her gently. 'Kate.'

A mumble what sounded like, 'Go 'way,' was her only response.

Only one thing for it, he thought, and began undoing the buttons on her blouse. His fingers fumbled as he revealed more of her flesh with each button he loosened. Light caressed the shadowy cleft between her breasts. He didn't intend to but his gaze flicked to her navel. No ruby—just a neat little hollow. His groin tightened as he remembered his fantasies that revolved around that particular part of her anatomy.

He willed it away and continued his task. It was impossible to remove her blouse further without disturbing her so he forced his gaze away from her bared flesh and lacy bra and searched for the skirt's zip. He slid it as far as he could, then eased her skirt down the long length of her shapely legs and off. Pulled a light sheet over her.

The sound of a phone ringing startled the daylights out of him—guilty conscience about the way his thoughts were going? He reached down to Kate's handbag, pulled out the offending item and lifted it to his ear. 'Kate Fielding's phone.'

'Who's this?' demanded a gruff voice.

'Damon Gillespie.'

'What are you doing in my daughter's room—it's what time over there?'

'About midnight, sir.' Three a.m. in Sydney. What prompted a man to ring his daughter at three o'clock in the morning? And answering her phone probably hadn't been a wise decision. 'Ah…we got in late. Kate left her phone…on the front desk and I picked it up and forgot to give it to her.'

'Katerina didn't ring to let us know she'd arrived safely.'

'Yes, we're here in Bali and everything's fine. I'm sure she's safely tucked up in bed and asleep so I won't wake her now.' He glanced at Kate, who hadn't stirred. 'I'll let her know you called…when I see her in the morning. Goodnight now.' He disconnected, set the phone on the night stand where she'd see it.

*Katerina.* Exquisite. He murmured the name aloud, linking it with the woman next to him as he watched her sleep. There was a lot he didn't know about Kate.

It occurred to him how little he really knew about the people in his life. Beyond business associates, few could be called friends because often he didn't stay around long enough to form lasting relationships.

Apart from their simmering sexual attraction could he call what he had with Kate friendship? Perhaps. But the term implied a mutual trust, openness and honesty that neither of them seemed to be prepared to share.

It implied a relationship built over time, something ongoing and into the future. His jaw hardened at the thought and he steeled the piece of his heart that had softened over the past few moments. No way was he going down that road again.

Pushing off the bed, he strode to his bag, stripped down to briefs, rummaged for his toiletries and went to take a cold shower.

Kate surfaced slowly. Images flitted in and out of her mind—falling disgracefully at Damon's feet, spewing her guts out in the bathroom. *'Oh, great,'* she groaned, rolling over and pressing her face into the pillow. Except for a gnawing feeling that strongly resembled hunger, she felt fine now.

Until she remembered what had happened just before she'd lost consciousness.

*Mr and Mrs Gillespie?* She rolled onto her back and opened her eyes. It was broad daylight and she was alone. In a big double bed. She stared at the rumpled expanse of sheets. Had he *planned* these sleeping arrangements? She thought he'd looked confused at the desk—or angry—but she'd been more concerned with maintaining an upright position to pay much attention.

And if not, why hadn't he then requested the hotel give them separate rooms? He'd obviously been here all night—she could smell his lingering presence. His watch lay on the night stand alongside her mobile phone. She shivered with a heat that all too often consumed her when she thought of Damon and her sleeping together in the true sense of the word. Too close, too intimate.

As she shifted position the sheet slipped and she drew in a short choppy breath. Her skirt was gone, her blouse completely unbuttoned…

Another shiver rippled through her. Damon. Had. Undressed. Her. He'd slid those big hands over her hips and pulled down her skirt. Grazed her breasts while undoing her buttons… The thought of him seeing her—like this—while asleep made her feel far too vulnerable.

And now he was nowhere to be seen.

Just like Nick when he'd betrayed and humiliated her with

another woman while she'd slept. The real and very private reason their relationship had ended.

It was the reason she slept alone. The reason she told herself she didn't want to be that close to anyone ever again. And that vulnerability had kept her lonely and alone on too many nights to count. Not that she was counting. She *didn't* want what Rosa was destined to have—a family of her own. She *didn't* want a man who loved her unreservedly.

So why the desperate lonely ache in her heart at the thought?

She slipped out of bed. She needed to look presentable in fresh clothes without bed hair and yesterday's grime on her skin when she saw Damon again. And *working*.

She took a quick shower, barely noticing the luxurious facilities. She semi-blow-dried her hair, leaving it damp and down, brushed her teeth, applied a light make-up, then redressed in a lime-green sundress with tiny yellow and white daisies. She grabbed her laptop, which she found with the rest of her stuff.

On her way out she noticed Damon's gear stowed beside a couch where he'd obviously spent at least part of the night. So maybe he hadn't planned this room arrangement. Or was it because she'd been of no use to anyone last night, herself included? What would have happened if she hadn't been ill?

*You know exactly what.*

She passed an aquamarine pool set amongst lush foliage, but didn't see Damon amongst the swimmers. The tempting aroma of hot food at the open-air restaurant teased her nostrils, but she had to find Damon first.

She saw him through the gym's floor-to-ceiling windows. He was bare-chested, wearing black and purple Lycra bike shorts and speeding nowhere on an exercise cycle. Sweat dampened his hair and glistened on his face and body. Angled away, he didn't see her, which gave Kate a rare opportunity to watch him unobserved. The way the muscles in his thighs and arms bunched and flexed, what she could see of his face in profile, a study in intense concentration.

He slowed as she watched, then dismounted and walked to a bench. Wow. Her gaze dropped to the bike shorts—rather, what was hidden in the bike shorts. *Not so hidden.* Heat coursed through her body, responding to the memory of just how impressive he'd been in the flesh. Inside her. The heat drained to her legs, making her feel weak-kneed, and she leaned against the wall.

Then he swiped a towel over his face and upper arms, picked up a shirt, shrugging it on as he smiled at someone across the room. Kate's gaze followed his. A woman. Tall, blonde, attractive. They gravitated towards each other and spoke, but Kate couldn't hear on the other side of the glass. Here less than a day and already he was chatting up the other guests. Just like Nick.

Her heart clenched. Too familiar. Too painful. She forced down the welling anger and humiliation that threatened to engulf her. Told herself she'd put her emotions on hold. What did she care? She should be used to coming second. This was *not* a holiday. Her fingers tightened on her laptop. This was *work*.

Damon and Blondie were still talking when she dragged herself away and found a quiet corner table in the open-air all-you-can-eat buffet on the other side of the path, opened her laptop and a new Word document.

So she wasn't watching twenty-seven minutes later when he stepped out of the sunshine and into the café—alone—with his shirt hanging open and his arms and bare chest gleaming with sweat. Nor when he caught sight of her and made his way towards her table.

'Kate. How are you feeling?'

She flicked a glance up at him. 'Good morning.' Then resumed tapping the keyboard with no idea what she was typing.

'You okay?'

'Fine now, thank you. A touch of food poisoning, I think.'

He stopped her with a hand on her wrist. Heat from his fingers zinged up her forearm. 'What are you doing?'

'Working. You should be too.' She glanced at her watch, then more pointedly at the paler band of flesh above his wrist. 'It's eleven a.m. Not that you'd know.'

He sat down with a frown. 'For Pete's sake, Kate. You were at death's door last night, be kind to yourself. And what are you expecting me to do on our first morning?'

*Our first morning.* He made it sound like they were on their honeymoon. She shifted uncomfortably. 'You could be quizzing the concierge about…things. Or making a formal complaint about the room debacle.' She stared at him over her computer.

He cocked a brow. 'What makes you think I haven't?'

She resumed typing. 'Because you've been too busy in the gym.'

The dig seemed to sail over his head. 'I spoke with management last night,' he continued. 'The problem should be sorted out by this afternoon.'

'Oh.' So why did she feel a horrible sense of disappointment in the pit of her stomach? *Stupid.* Not disappointment—jet lag and lack of food, she told herself. She did *not* want to spend the next nine nights sleeping in a double suite with Damon. Not at all.

'So you're okay now?' he asked again.

'Yes. I seem to have purged myself of whatever it was.'

'Good.' He pushed up. 'I'll get us some sustenance.'

She shook her head. 'I'm not hungry.' *I'm too busy being ridiculously, irrationally mad.*

'Something plain, then. You should try to eat.'

A few moments later he returned with a tray. He set a tiny Chinese cup of clear green tea and a plate with a single bread roll and an apple in front of her. He'd selected an assortment of pastries and one temptingly fragrant cup of coffee for himself.

The fact that he'd remembered her saying she preferred tea first thing in the morning irritated her more. Her staccato tapping increased in tempo.

He tore a piece off his pineapple Danish. 'Kate, anyone

with half a brain can see you're not typing constructively so I take it you're ticked off with me about the room.'

Very carefully, very calmly, she switched off her computer, closed it. 'If you say the room business is sorted, that's fine. Great.' She reached for her tea and concentrated on its fragrance as she brought it to her lips.

'So it's not the room.' He leaned forward, so close she could see a tiny muscle twitch at the side of his mouth. 'Let's get it out in the open now—I don't fancy spending the next week with an uptight, inflexible, non-communicative woman.'

She reared back. Uptight, non-communicative right now—maybe. But, 'Inflexible?' she snapped. 'Who are you calling inflexible? Haven't we all bent over backwards to accommodate your ideas? Isn't that why I'm here in Bali? Because you want *your* staff to be able to speak with experience?' Setting her cup down, she pushed away from the table and rose. She wasn't going to sit here and let Damon Arrogance Gillespie throw stones at her. 'You want honest and open communication, you start first.'

Damon curled the hand that had belatedly shot out to restrain her, and replaced it firmly on the table. He'd never run after a woman; he refused to do so now. He watched her walk away, her head high, back stiff as starch. Damn right she was uptight. But she'd managed to communicate her displeasure loud and clear.

His last mouthful of pastry, still unchewed, lodged behind his Adam's apple like a fistful of soggy cardboard. Why had he just acted like a supercilious jerk?

Because he'd never met a woman like Kate Fielding before.

She did things to him he'd never experienced. Whatever it was, it was something new. He let the knowledge roll around in his mind and settle. It wasn't only her body he wanted. Kate was more interesting—and more complicated—than any woman he'd ever known.

He genuinely liked her. He liked her mind, the way she

cared about other people. She was responsible, dependable, and… flexible. And she expected the same from those around her. So he'd give her a moment. Then he'd go find her and they'd talk. Calmly. Without the knot in his throat.

Ten minutes later he hesitated outside their door, unsure whether to walk straight in. So he knocked before entering. He found her standing on the balcony looking out at the sea. The breeze played with her hair, and even from the other side of the room he could smell its fresh citrus fragrance.

She looked tiny and vulnerable and impossibly young in that whimsical little-girl dress framed by the dark floor-to-ceiling slatted doors. A thread of remorse tugged at his conscience. 'Kate.'

She didn't turn around so he couldn't read her mood on her face, but the starch had gone from her posture and her hands were curled against her sides.

When she remained as she was, he stopped a couple of paces behind her. 'Look at me, Kate.'

He saw her hands tighten, and when she turned there was no trace of vulnerability he might have imagined he'd see in her expression. But over-bright eyes betrayed her. Anger? Hurt? Or a determined pride to face him on her terms. He didn't know; all he knew was it tore him up inside.

Purely unintentionally, his gaze dipped to the curve of her breasts, her slim waist and down to perfectly shaped legs visible through the thin fabric—and despite the cool salty breeze his blood turned hot.

He forced his eyes back to hers. 'I want you, Kate.' His heart beat oddly when he said her name.

She shook her head, swiping at tears, and he could tell she was mad as hell about them. He wasn't aware of taking those last couple of steps, but suddenly he was hauling her willowy body against his, loving the plumpness of her breasts against his chest, the way her small frame fitted against him.

'No.' She struggled to free herself from his grasp. 'Not with unresolved tension between us.'

He wiped the moisture from below her lashes with his thumbs and, looking deep into those midnight eyes, he said, 'It'll be okay, Kate, I'll make it okay. All the way okay. Just tell me what's wrong.'

And he lowered his lips to hers, sliding his fingers beneath her hair so he could cradle her head in his palm and know, *feel*, she wanted this as much as he. For a beat out of time his lips tingled with her taste as her mouth softened beneath his.

Then she pushed at him again, jerking them out of the moment and sucking in air. 'You don't want me—you just want sex.'

Desire sparked bright and hot in her eyes. 'If we're talking honest and open here, that's what we both want,' he said calmly and with absolute certainty.

Her nostrils flared at that as she drew in a sharp breath and drilled a finger into his chest. 'Guys like you always think sex is the answer.'

He smiled, safe in the knowledge that some of her steam had evaporated since her voice had lost its hard edge and taken on a husky tone. 'What happened to make love not war? It always works for me.' Until he moved on. 'And what do you mean by *guys like me*?'

She frowned. 'Guys who…you know damn well what I mean.'

He shrugged, which earned him a glare. 'I'm not sure I do.'

She had him pegged. But for some reason where Kate was concerned, he didn't feel the self-image fitted as well as it always had. Unsettling.

The glare stayed in place. Risking retribution, he reached out and stroked her cheek. 'And if you think sex is all I want from you, Kate, you're wrong.'

She made a point of looking at his engorged Lycra-covered crotch, which proved him a liar.

'Hey, give a guy a break.' He just knew he shouldn't have worn bike shorts this morning. 'I never said I didn't want sex, I said it wasn't all I wanted from you.' Yet perhaps the fact that she could see how physically aroused he was could work in his favour. 'What's more, I'll prove it to you.'

A pause, then a rusty, 'Yeah, right, and how exactly do you propose to do that?'

'By *not* having sex with you.'

That threw her, he thought, with little satisfaction to his personal discomfort. The vertical crease between her brows was back. She blinked up at him, disappointment creeping into her eyes as she processed his words. 'I didn't—'

'You can't have it both ways, Kate.'

Her mouth remained slightly parted as if she intended to finish whatever she'd been saying, but she must have thought better of it.

He watched her turn away to face the sea once more, her arms folded across her chest. She wasn't the only one disappointed. Before he'd thought it through, his mouth had run away from the rest of him. And the rest of him howled a stiff protest.

But he'd made the right decision. Actions spoke louder than any words. Or, in this instance, inaction.

'I'm going to take a shower,' he said. 'Then after we've had our little talk, if you're feeling up to it we could go exploring. Or laze around the pool—whatever you're comfortable with.'

She didn't turn around. 'That's your choice for today's activity?'

*Not even close.* 'Whatever you want's fine by me.' Turning away, he moved to his gear, pulled out a pair of shorts and a T-shirt.

'Didn't you mention risk-taking and adventure?'

He yanked off his sneakers. 'You've been ill. I won't push you into anything strenuous today. We can call a dip in the pool water sports if you want. By the way, a guest in the gym this morning was asking after you.' He padded towards the bathroom. 'She saw you faint in the lobby last night and said to tell you if you don't trust foreign doctors she has her own practice in Perth. She's in room thirty-three.'

Kate heard the bathroom door close, then rubbed at her arms to mask the flesh made sensitive by Damon's hands as she stared at the shimmer of sand and sea. So Blondie was a doctor. Now she felt like an idiot for thinking the worst about him and the woman in the gym. The sound of running water only intensified the whirlpool of conflicting emotions.

He wasn't Nick. He wasn't anything like Nick. But she refused to let him callously reel off her shortcomings in one minute, and kiss her senseless the next.

She tried not to think about what she was missing out on. Wall-to-wall marble bathroom. Damon. A stack of luxury products designed to soothe and pamper, gliding over skin and muscle.

Damon. Naked. Soaping up with those products under the double shower heads. All that bronzed skin glistening with water and oils… If she just walked in…would he change his mind? Her pulse rate picked up pace. *Should she?* She bit her lip. She was never indecisive. Clear and level-headed in any situation.

Not this particular one.

And if she did choose to follow him into the shower, one-night stand aside, it would never be the same between them again.

*It would be more,* an inner voice whispered.

Until he went back to wherever he came from, she warned that inner voice. Disentangling her arms, she crossed the room, rummaged in the bottom of her bag for the supply of condoms she'd carefully packed beneath her clothes, then kicked off her sandals.

Office hours did *not* apply in Bali.

# CHAPTER NINE

KATE knocked once, then when there was no reply she eased the door open a fraction and called, 'Damon?'

The fragrance of something cool and green wafted to her nose. The sound of the water reminded her of a tropical rainstorm as she peeked tentatively around the door and said, 'Damon?' again.

She caught sight of him behind the water-spattered glass. He was rinsing his hair, and, oh, my…goodness. Even slightly blurred she could see he was perfect. The lighting gilded his skin, highlighting strong facial planes and angles. Dark masculine hair spattered his broad chest and arrowed down a washboard stomach to… Wow.

She swallowed as everything inside her liquefied. Her legs seized up, nailing her to the spot when she would have stepped back. Out. Away. Whatever was she thinking, coming in here?

*You know exactly what,* her now cheerful inner voice said. She'd made up her mind. Be it a holiday or an educational, whatever this trip was, right now they were a world away from home and family, business and work colleagues. Consequences didn't enter into it. She knew what she was getting herself into. Didn't she?

He ran his hands through his hair, gave his head a shake, scattering drops, then glanced her way. His expression didn't change, as if he was accustomed to women joining him in the bathroom unannounced. 'Kate?'

She jerked her eyes to his. Then to the bird-of-paradise floral arrangement on the vanity. Her legs turned from unresponsive to jelly and she sank to the side of the spa. 'I have a question.'

'You have a question,' he repeated. 'It couldn't wait until I finished?'

'Actually, no.' She forced herself to meet his eyes. *Only* his eyes. 'When you said you're not going to have sex with me…do you mean ever?'

Barely letting his eyes stray, he selected a bottle of something, squeezed a dollop into his hand. 'I meant now.' He rubbed the liquid between his palms together slowly. A muscle clenched in his jaw and the topaz colour in his gaze smouldered, but his voice didn't waver when he said, 'So I suggest you leave. While you still can.'

The thought of her being the cause of him losing that cool control scorched its way down her body, making her pulse heavy, her blood syrupy. 'I was thinking—um—we could maybe try the "make love not war" thing and see if it works for us.'

'Kate,' he warned, his voice thickening. 'I'm not kidding here.'

'Nor am I.' She opened her hand and showed him the condom packet. Then she rose, reached behind and unzipped her dress. Slipped the straps off her shoulders and let it drop to the floor. 'You mentioned water sports?'

She saw him swallow as his eyes slid over her now semi-naked body. He squeezed more lotion onto his hands.

She could tell he wasn't thinking much beyond the moment. Neither was she, but she did remember, 'You said whatever I wanted was fine by you.' She unhooked her bra, tossed it onto the vanity. Sliding her palms down her hips, she shimmied out of her panties.

He swore.

She laughed. And chalked it up to nervousness. *That's exactly right, Kate. Keep it flirty, keep it fun.*

She opened the glass door and stepped into the shower stall with him. Her breath caught, the condom slipped out of her hand and a squeal shot up her throat. 'It's cold!' She jerked away, but was immediately hauled back under the spray by one strong arm.

'You're the reason it's cold,' Damon murmured, his hot breath a stark contrast against her neck, just below her ear lobe. 'Too late to back out now—your fate's sealed.'

As if to underscore his words, he placed an open-mouthed kiss where he'd spoken, closed his teeth over the spot and bit down gently. Possessively. Damp, warm, erotic—he smooched his way down the side of her throat, nipping and sucking while one hand reached out to adjust the water's temperature to a degree or two above body heat.

He shifted close, meltingly close, so that the full length of their naked bodies touched for the very first time, and her breath caught again; with wonder. She'd never had a lover so tall. So broad. So overwhelming. She'd never felt so tiny as she did within Damon's aura of masculinity.

The beat of the water added another sensation to the layers already thrumming through her body. Amazing sensations. The heat of his body and the coolness of the marble tiles beneath her feet. His hardness against her softer curves. The exotic scent as he smoothed lotion-slick hands over her shoulders, then slowly down her back as if counting each rib as he went.

His mouth reached the hollow above her collarbone as his hands reached her buttocks to tuck her hard up against him. And 'Aah…'

His answering groan rumbled deep in his chest, vibrating against her flesh. Tingling against her nipples. Then words, thought, incoherent sounds, faded into a whirlpool of need as he turned with her so that she stood against the tiles. She found herself being lifted, her back in contact with the marble, two strong arms circling her waist as if she weighed nothing and a muscled hairy thigh supporting her. Devastatingly intimate.

Eye to eye, mouth to mouth. Heat to heat. Breathing turned short and choppy, then impossible as his mouth swooped to hers. His tongue demanded entry, plunging between her softened and sensitive lips. Wild and wet. Again that overwhelming feeling that he was perhaps too much man for her to handle.

Odd, since the first time they'd had sex she hadn't felt that way. But that had been a brief frantic encounter metres away from a roomful of people. Here, buck naked and without Shakira's veiled anonymity, it was different. In lots of ways. But the most important one was that they knew one another better now.

Oh, but some things hadn't changed, she thought hazily while she surrendered against him. The friction of his body on hers. The sensation of his hands on her willing flesh as he explored her breasts, tweaking her nipples into hard, sensitised peaks and sending need spiralling low in her abdomen. His taste, his unique scent, the urgency that ignited between them whenever they touched.

The hard ridge of his erection nudged against her thigh. She squirmed against it, arching her hips and driving herself to a ragged edge, clutching at his shoulders only to have her fingers skate away over a film of soapsuds.

Suddenly he slapped his hands against the tiles on either side of her head, leaving her weight supported only by the thigh pressed between hers, and stared down at her. She was surprised the heat in his eyes didn't turn the water on her skin to steam.

Then he wrenched off the taps beside her head and stepped back, letting her slide bonelessly down the shower stall until her feet hit the tiles. 'I promised I wouldn't over-tire you today,' he murmured, his voice deep, husky.

'I'm feeling better every minute,' she assured him.

He reached for a towel, his eyes still holding hers. 'No. I think you need to lie down.'

'Oh… Yes… Maybe…'

'Definitely.' He wrapped the towel around her, patting and stroking her through its soft terry fabric, trailing warmth and excitement everywhere he rubbed. He retrieved the condom from the floor, then somehow she was in his arms being carried towards the massive bed.

He laid her on her back, knelt on the bed straddling her, his knees imprisoning her outer thighs. 'Lie still and relax,' he ordered softly. 'This might take a while.'

He unwrapped her slowly as if opening a gift. Every inch of skin he exposed shimmered with heat, quivered in anticipation. His eyes were so potent it was as if they touched her. Caressed her. Explored every naked inch of her. The pleasure was like nothing she'd ever felt before. And building with every thump of her heart.

'You have the most amazing body, Kate.'

She thought she saw something deeper in his molten honey gaze and willed away the flash of disappointment—had she expected him to say more? This wasn't about feelings or emotion, she reminded herself. This was about lust—only lust, and temporary at that. She smiled up at him, then let her gaze drift down. 'You're not so bad yourself.'

Impossible not to let her eyes linger. Droplets of water glistened on his skin and clung to the coarse masculine hair that spattered his chest. She wanted to lean up on her elbows and place her lips on the pulse she could see beating at his throat, but right now a glorious lethargy claimed her. All she was capable of was arching back against the soft terry towel and letting out a sigh that sounded more like a purr.

Until the slow and thorough sweep of his gaze alone was no longer enough. 'Damon…'

'Shh,' he whispered, lowering his head. 'I told you to relax.'

She surrendered to the sensation of his teeth tugging oh-solightly on a nipple while his hands stroked her arms from shoulder to fingertips, from collarbone to the curve of her waist, then finally moulded around her breasts. Gentle and persuasive, light but with a powerful domination that made her weak.

*Not* relaxing. Her pulse rate doubled, her body cried out for more. But her feebly voiced protest was useless, ignored. And it really wasn't a protest—more of a whimper. Of need. She closed her eyes as his mouth and hands and body journeyed lower and his tongue dipped into her navel. Lower. But when his breath brushed the apex of her thighs her hand shot down to grasp his hair. 'I…'

He glanced up at her. 'What's wrong?'

'I… No one's ever…' She trailed off, unable to speak.

An incredulous expression lit his face. 'No one?'

She could barely shake her head. Not even the man she'd been going to marry had been so intimate with her. Sex had been good with Nick, but he wasn't really a guy to look after a woman's needs. Not hers, at any rate.

Damon, on the other hand… His gaze warmed, large blunt fingers pried her legs apart. 'Then I'm the first.'

Her hand tightened on his hair, but she didn't pull him away. Ooh. The first sweep of his tongue over her moist centre and she saw stars—bright, pulsing and white-hot. The second time and she quite simply flew apart. Ignited. Erupted. Exploded.

It was probably several seconds before she floated down from wherever he'd shot her breathless and gasping, to the relative sanity of their room and the slow-moving draught of tropical air provided by the overhead fan.

And Damon. Ripping open the foil packet, sheathing himself before easing inside her, slick, hot and hard, his gaze locked with hers, his arms quivering slightly supporting his weight above her.

Drawing her still-spasming muscles tight around him, she pressed her heels into his buttocks, grasped the smooth roundness of his shoulders and moved with him, spiralling towards the stars once more.

They crested the peak together. 'Oh. My. God.' Kate closed her eyes as they coasted down the other side. 'I think I just hit the jackpot.'

'Twice.' Damon sounded pleased. And smug.

'Another first,' she felt duty-bound to tell him as he rolled off her. Though why she thought he deserved to know such a detail was a mystery to her.

He propped his head on an upturned palm to watch her, his free hand drawing lazy circles on her stomach. 'You amaze me, *Katerina*.'

Her breath caught at his use of her full name. When her father used it, it sounded abrupt and formal. Damon's husky low voice, the way he drew it out over four syllables, made it sound beautiful, desirable.

'So I'm assuming Dad rang last night.'

'Yes.' A lopsided smile creased one cheek as he spoke. 'He wondered what I was doing in his daughter's room.'

She almost smiled back. 'I'm guessing you didn't enlighten him.'

'I told him you'd left your phone at the desk and that you'd ring him back. I take it you haven't.'

'Not yet.' And she didn't feel inclined to at the moment. Said moment lost some of its sparkle as other emotions intruded, tarnishing the glow. Guilt because she should have rung home already. Irritation because she didn't want to think about her family for the next few days. The countdown was on, the hours until they went back to their respective working lives in Sydney were ticking away. And she wanted to enjoy every precious but fleeting second.

'He was concerned for you,' Damon said, interpreting her expression correctly. 'The way every parent should be.'

There was a fleeting wistfulness in his tone and Kate immediately remembered Damon's mum and dad and their total lack of parental care. 'I know.' She shrugged. 'But I'm thirty years old.'

'Any parent worth his salt doesn't stop worrying just because his kid grows up. Allow him the privilege of caring about you, Kate. Don't give him cause to worry.'

She reached out to trail a finger down his chest, around his navel to the thicker hair below, and batted wide, innocent eyes at him. 'A bit late for that, isn't it—you don't think the past little while here on this bed would give him good cause?'

His half-grin didn't quite erase the serious glint in his eyes. 'Ring him, that's all I'm saying.'

'I will. Later. After we've eaten.' She leaned over and reached for the room-service menu. 'My appetite's back and right now I'm starving.'

Half an hour later they were enjoying a mid-afternoon snack. Clear chicken soup flavoured with lemon grass and shallots, followed by a traditional Balinese dish of yellow rice called *nasi kuning* accompanied by grilled fish in banana leaves. All set out in the middle of the bed.

'You know your way around a Balinese menu,' she said, licking oil off her fingers. 'Have you been here before?'

He scooped up a mouthful of rice. 'I've spent a lot of time in this part of the world.'

'What made you leave Australia?'

He stopped chewing and the relaxed man she'd shared the meal with seemed to disappear behind a sombre façade. His posture stiffened, and his voice was flatly remote when he said, 'There was nothing holding me there.'

Kate sensed there was more to it, something he couldn't or wouldn't share. 'Not your grandmother? Bryce?'

'Bryce and I had nothing in common any more. And Gran…' He trailed off, staring towards the balcony and out to sea and Kate saw no lingering fondness she'd have expected in his gaze. 'She'd done what she saw as a duty and I'm forever grateful to her for that. It was time to move on.' He set his plate aside. 'Have you seen much of Asia, Kate?'

Damon knew he'd left Kate with more questions than

answers, that his response had told her nothing. That he was turning the conversation to her. He didn't want to relive the pain of old wounds. Bonita had been the only person he'd loved unconditionally and he'd long ago accepted that Gran had never loved him.

'Quite a bit. Damon…'

He saw those questions in her eyes. Eyes that reminded him too much of other eyes, other times. His jaw locked tight. He would *not* revisit those times. For anyone.

She reached out a hand to touch his, but he withdrew, preferring to stack their dishes on the tray and set it on the floor than risk anything remotely emotional. If he wasn't careful he was going to fall for Kate harder than he intended to and he refused to let that to happen. Fun—temporary—times were all he'd allow himself.

She shrugged his response off, but there was hurt behind the sting in her voice. 'We need to get some things straight before we go back to work. Our relationship, for a start—'

'We've got ten days, Kate—nine now. Don't think about work. Or the future. What would you do if you only had those nine days?'

She frowned. 'What sort of pessimistic outlook is that?'

'Humour me. Think about it.'

'I'd spend it with my family.'

'And if it was just the two of us? Here?'

Her brow wrinkled in thought. 'You're saying what we have here, now, is all we have?'

He continued looking into her eyes. 'Don't think beyond next week.'

'So to our talk we didn't get around to… You're saying lovers without strings, no delving into personal history, no getting emotionally involved. Just us and good times. For nine more days. Have I got it right?'

'We'll have fun, Kate.'

She nodded slowly. 'Fun. But no sleepovers.'

He thought about that for a moment. 'You mean you're kicking me out? After what we just shared? Enjoyed?'

Her expression was resolute. 'Yes.'

'How will that look—the guy slipping out to another room every night in the wee hours?'

To his surprise, her gaze turned inward as if remembering something before she seemed to collect her thoughts and made what appeared to be a darn hard effort to smile. 'I turn into a pumpkin at midnight.'

She was probably right, but not about the pumpkin. Yes, they needed some privacy, some time apart—being together 24/7 for nine days might be overdoing it—but there was more going on here. 'What did he do to you?'

Her gaze flickered a moment. 'Who?'

'I'm asking *you*, Kate.'

She looked away. 'My ex-fiancé. Nick. He made a fool of me. Didn't we just agree to no personal history?'

Damon touched her cheek, turned her face towards him, wanting to erase the sadness in her eyes, wanting to ease the vulnerability he read there. 'He was the fool, Kate, not you.'

'Yes, well… I'm wiser now. I'm not interested in long term.' Shaking her head, she made an effort to sound upbeat, closing the discussion with, 'So is the daytime-night-time activities thingy still on?'

She'd never make a good poker player. 'Yes.' He smiled into her eyes. 'I've planned tomorrow already.'

'Have you now?' It was her turn to smile. Wickedly. She shifted towards him, then rose up on her knees to slide her lush mouth over his. 'I've got tonight planned as well.'

'Ah,' Kate murmured the following day as they left the hotel lobby and approached the gleaming Harley-Davidson motorbike Damon had hired for the afternoon. 'This'll be a new experience.'

'Yeah,' he murmured, admiring her fitted white calf-length trousers and sapphire top, her dark hair braided close to her head. They'd spent last night exploring each other—until he'd trundled down the hall to his own room—now it was time to explore Bali. And he'd have that body snug against him all the way.

He handed her a helmet, then retrieved a couple of heavy leather jackets from the back of the bike and held one out to her. 'You'll need this for protection.'

'Okay…' The thing swamped her and her brow wrinkled as she shrugged it on. 'I look ridiculous.'

'No.' He reached out to pull it together and fasten the zip. His knuckles grazed her firm, flat abdomen and the curve of her breasts as he tugged the zipper slowly to her neck and lingered there a second or two enjoying the sweet warmth of her pulse while watching her dark eyes frowning into his. 'You look sexy. Adorably sexy.'

Her eyes turned black and for a moment the thought of going back to her room was a sizzling possibility, but she pulled on her helmet, and the eye contact was lost. 'Do you have a destination in mind?'

'Yes.' He straddled the bike, holding it steady while she climbed on behind him.

'Are you going to fill me in?'

'Not yet. Just hold on tight, lean into me and move with the bike and you'll be fine.'

'Okay.'

Damon kept it sedate, giving her time to adjust to the bike and an opportunity to enjoy the local scenery. The wind sneaked through his visor as he picked up speed and turned onto a road off the beaten tourist track following the coast in a westerly direction.

Kate's breasts were pressed hard against his back—he could feel her shape through the leather jacket. Her inner thighs hugged his hips. He liked the way her hands gripped his jacket, liked the feeling of sharing the moment with her, as if they were the only two people in the world. He hadn't experienced that feeling in a long time.

Eventually he drew to a stop near a break in the foliage, killed the engine and removed his helmet. 'Take a look.'

Through tropical green palms a brilliant lapis sea scrolled over stunning volcanic black sand. A sheltered cove, deserted and private. He'd discovered this place on a previous trip, but sharing it with Kate was like seeing it through new eyes.

'My black sand beach.' He heard her sigh of approval as she unwrapped her hands and lifted the helmet from her head. 'It's spectacular.'

'You need to experience it up close,' he said, unloading the small cooler pack containing Asian spring rolls and a bottle of water. Grabbing her hand, he led her through the palms that dipped almost to the water's edge.

Kate breathed deeply, drawing the humidity with its scent of the beach into her lungs. Not another living soul to be seen. All this sand, all that water, and just her and Damon to share it. Alone.

Damon unzipped his jacket; she did the same. They sat, yanked off their shoes. Then he surged up, tugged his T-shirt over his head and unsnapped the top of his jeans and grinned at her. Clearly he expected her to balk at the idea of stripping off.

'I can be adventurous,' she said with a lift of her chin. But she glanced about them nevertheless.

'Black beaches are not as popular.' He shucked his jeans. 'We've got the place to ourselves.'

She unbuttoned her top, but couldn't bring herself to take it off. 'I've got more to hide than you.'

He stripped off his jocks and with typical masculine confidence, said, 'That so?'

Her gaze took in every naked and impressive inch of him. *Okay, maybe not.* Her breath rasped out as her fingers paused at the waistband of her trousers. She swallowed. 'Is this today's adventure?'

He raised a brow. 'Not daring enough for you?'

She choked out a laugh. 'Oh, yeah, plenty enough.' Taking a breath, she shoved her jeans down her legs, kicked them aside. Shrugged out of her blouse. What *was* she doing, standing on a public beach like a frightened virgin in her chaste white lace underwear and staring at the buck-naked man in front of her?

A wickedly naked man with the most gorgeous body she'd ever seen. Who knew how to use that body on hers to full and glorious effect.

Her pulse was doing somersaults in her veins, not only because she was about to strip off on a public beach, but because the memory of last night's intimate encounter with that body was stunningly clear and real.

He set his hands on his hips. 'Last one in, then?'

She could smell the sun on his sweat-sheened skin. She'd be powerless to stop him seducing her into removing her underwear if he stepped any closer and this time she wanted to do it herself to show him she wasn't afraid of being naked with him in public.

Good Lord, *in public*. What happened to tourists arrested for indecent exposure under Indonesia's strict laws? Her fingers fumbled with her bra hook. 'Wait…' She tossed the garment onto the sand, pushed her panties down and stepped out of them. 'Last one in…does what?'

Before she could blink he was off and running into the water. Its deep blue colour rippled out around him as he grinned at her with a purely masculine glint of wickedness in his eyes. 'Come on in and I'll explain it to you.'

# CHAPTER TEN

THEY spent the following days visiting local markets, immersing themselves in Balinese culture at the numerous temples and enjoying its hospitality at a couple of relaxing massage and well-being centres. In the evenings they took in a couple of cultural shows, dropped in at a few night spots. And in between, they found time to enjoy the hotel's amenities—pool, spa. The luxurious double bed.

Kate lay awake in that bed now. Alone. Wondering why she sent him on his way every night when here, away from family, was the perfect opportunity to let him stay. He'd lain beside her after making love only an hour ago. The scent of their passion still lingered. It was so tempting to turn a blind eye to the fact that they had to return to their working lives the day after tomorrow.

But they'd both made it clear that this was all there was. All it could be—she didn't date her boss. He'd be gone in probably a matter of months, and hopefully she'd have had the chance to demonstrate she possessed the skills to run the centre by then.

His idea to expose her to new experiences seemed to have fallen by the wayside in favour of their enthusiasm for exploring each other. Perhaps he wasn't the reckless live-for-the-moment guy she'd initially thought when she'd seen him in his jungle gear. Bad boy to her good girl. She stared up at the slow-moving fan. First impressions could be wrong, couldn't they?

And he had his own share of secrets. Secrets that put shadows in his eyes and added a roughness to his voice when he'd turn away. He could talk all he liked about how he preferred his life uncomplicated and unencumbered or give her the impression he was free as a bird, but he didn't fool her.

For one, he cared about her, at least a little. He'd told her it wasn't just sex, and what was more he'd tried to prove it. Another, he cared about his uncle. She could see it now, whenever Bryce came up in conversation. They might not have been close, but the bond of family was still strong. Why stay to sort out Bryce's business when clearly he wanted to be some place else?

Some place he wasn't going to talk about with her.

Even though physically they were as intimate as two lovers could be, emotionally it was a different story. So he cared about her. That didn't mean he wouldn't walk away without a backward glance when the time came. His emotions, when it came to her, had a turn-off switch, whereas she was hopelessly out of her depth. Oh, she could play the siren for him—in fact, to her everlasting surprise, she'd discovered she could do it very well. But it was becoming harder and harder to keep her head above water.

Tomorrow was their last day on Bali. The past week had been the most memorable of her life, but she needed to start pulling away. Now.

Except… She remembered how he'd looked asleep just before she'd woken him up to turf him out. His face shadowed in the semi-darkness, muted light from beyond the suite's balcony soothing the strong jaw, the straight nose. His large hand resting possessively over her belly button. She could get seriously used to this.

And that was asking for a broken heart. Worse, her stupid heart didn't want to listen to her head.

Was she falling in love?

In love with a man who was going to walk away from her.

She shook her head against the pillow. No. No. No. Been there, done that, had the scars to prove it. She was never going to let herself be hurt like that again.

As they journeyed towards Damon's mystery destination for their final day, Kate saw several paraglider canopies high in the sky, circling like rainbow lorikeets through the car's windscreen. Her stomach clenched and she looked away quickly to concentrate on the stands of coconut palms and little temple coming into view. Much better.

But then the road began to climb the side of a hill and it became nauseatingly obvious when Damon came to a stop a short distance away from others with a similar death wish what his plans were. The sickening scenario washed through her and she clutched her hands together in her lap. 'I can't do that. I won't.'

'Come on, Kate, be a sport.' He opened his car door.

Kate remained where she was, every cell in her body revolting at the thought. She shook her head. 'I am *not* going up in one of those things. Nothing dangerous—you promised.' She looked across and met his eyes.

'We made a deal.' He smiled, his teeth white against his tan and a shadow of stubble. 'Kate, it's a tandem; you'll be with me. I've done it a hundred times.'

'*No.*' She shook her head, but her attention was momentarily diverted by a blond-haired man approaching. 'You know that guy?'

Damon waved at him. 'We met here a few years ago. He's an Aussie, he married a local. Hey, Seb.' He climbed out of the vehicle and shook hands, spoke for a few moments, then leaned in to her with a grin. 'This is Kate. She's a nervous first-timer. Perhaps you can put her at ease while I check my equipment.'

Seb slid into the driver's seat while Damon walked away in the direction of a low building. 'You'll be fine. Damo's an experienced pilot.'

'He tricked me into this. And I'm not about to cast my fate to the winds.'

'So what's a nice girl like you doing hooked up with a guy like Damo?' Seb said, ignoring her protest. 'Don't tell me he's finally settled down.'

The image Seb tossed out disturbed her in the extreme. Settle down with Damon? With a man who wanted her to fly off a cliff with him? 'A guy like Damon will never settle down. We work together, that's all. He's been here before?'

'A few times a year,' Seb said cheerfully.

'What does your wife think of you risking your life?' She glared at him, knowing she was being harsh, not caring. 'Throwing it away and not concerned about who you hurt in the process?' She hadn't realised her fingernails had dug grooves in her palms until she saw Seb staring at the slow ooze of blood.

'She often flies too, but with the baby…'

'A *baby*? You have a baby and you still do this?'

He shifted uncomfortably and peered through the windscreen obviously willing Damon to reappear and wishing himself somewhere else. 'It's not that big a deal.'

'No? Would you still say that if she fell to her death? If she left you to bring up your child alone?'

'Ah-h-h…here he comes.' Seb jumped out of the car as if he were on springs.

She watched him jog to Damon, who was carrying two helmets and a bunch of other stuff that looked way too flimsy to hold his weight, let alone the two of them. Seb shrugged. Damon frowned in her direction.

She glared back. Let him call her a coward. Let them both. Because they didn't know, men like them would never understand.

Until it was too late.

Leaning over, she grabbed the keys from the ignition, then pushed up and out of the car. At the sight of her approach, Seb gave a quick wave and made an even quicker getaway.

Damon dumped the paraphernalia at their feet. 'Kate. It'll be okay.' He wrapped his arms around her. His scent permeated her senses. His hard, warm body pressed against the quivering length of hers. Alive, so alive and vibrant and vital. For now. How easy to allow herself to be seduced into changing her mind.

'You can't guarantee that.' She pushed away from him and stared into his eyes, but she couldn't see them properly because her own were blurred. Damon wasn't the only one haunted by old grief. 'Risk your life, then. I'm going back to the hotel.'

His smile faded, replaced by a cool demeanour. 'You're being over-dramatic, Kate.' He picked up a helmet and put it on, slid on his sunglasses.

'You think?' She jingled the car keys in front of him. 'My brother died throwing himself off a cliff in a hang-glider. I won't stand around and watch someone else I l—' she caught the runaway word on her tongue '—someone else who thinks he's invincible prove he's flesh and blood and as easily broken as the rest of us mere mortals.'

A moment of stunned silence hummed in the air before anger and desperation gave way to an all too familiar bone-deep weariness.

'Just go away and do your thing.' She turned on her heel and pointed herself in the direction of their car, but she only made it halfway before Damon clapped his hands on her shoulders.

He spun her to face him. 'Kate.'

Sunlight glinted off his helmet. She couldn't see his eyes behind his sunglasses so she couldn't read his expression. Glaring up at the mirrored lenses, the firm, implacable, *fragile* jaw, she fought back tears. 'Get out of my way.'

'No.' Damon yanked off his helmet and glasses, tossed them on the ground. A ball of something like guilt hit him square in his gut as he closed his fingers around the slender bones of Kate's upper arms, drew her shivering body against his. He buried his nose against the soft fragrance of her hair. He'd never felt so inadequate.

Yes, he had—and his fingers tightened on her arms as he remembered. When he'd watched Bonita die.

He understood Kate's anguish. And realised how differently they'd dealt with their loss. It had made her afraid to take risks, whereas he'd used risk to block out the pain. He released her arms to stroke her shoulders, her neck, the sun-warmed braid against her back.

She jutted her chin up at him. 'Doesn't the word *death* mean anything to you?'

He shook his head. 'Death only makes you more aware of your own mortality. It reminds us to live for today because we never know when it might be our last.' A creed he'd lived by every day for the past nine years. He focused directly into her eyes. 'Are you a woman who likes to live each day to the full?'

Her eyes widened fractionally and her posture stiffened. 'I like to *live*, yes.'

'*Carpe diem*, Kate. Seize the day.' He tightened his fingers around her slender bones, felt the telltale tremor run through her. 'You can do this—not for me; for *you*.'

Her eyelids closed and two fat tears rolled down her cheeks. He wiped them away with his thumbs. 'You face this and overcome it, you'll feel a freedom you've never felt.'

She seemed to wage some sort of internal battle, then straightened, and when she opened her eyes a light glimmered that hadn't been there two minutes earlier.

He added a gentle squeeze of reassurance. 'Believe in yourself, Kate.'

A good fifteen seconds of silence passed. 'You'll owe me big time,' she murmured finally.

She flashed that tiny spark of courage at him and he felt as if he'd lost an already tenuous foothold on the side of the mountain.

Whether she knew it or not, Kate Fielding had Power. The

power to do whatever she chose, if she'd just reach out and seize it. He bent down to retrieve their gear. He had a feeling that if she chose to wield that power—over him—she had way more than was safe.

But her lips were chalk-white and clamped together as he slid the helmet over her head. 'Hey, it's like sex,' he reassured her, tracing those lips with a finger. 'We fly off the edge of the world and—'

'I'll scream,' she warned him between clenched teeth. 'And possibly pass out. Are you ready for that?'

'Ready, willing and able.' He grinned. 'As I said, it's like sex. Spectacular, *swoon-worthy* sex.'

'I don't scream when I'm having sex.'

A smile twitched at his cheeks as he checked over the equipment a final time. 'Perhaps you should.'

'Is that a criticism?'

His grin widened. 'You should let yourself go—you don't do enough of that. Or maybe I'm just not doing my job well enough.'

He didn't miss the momentary heat flare in her eyes, but her voice remained cool as she said, 'If you're fishing for compliments, forget it.'

He resumed his task. 'Okay, let's buckle up. No loose items in pockets?' She shook her head. 'Put your sunglasses on.' One knuckle grazed the soft, sweet valley between her breasts as he lifted the glasses hooked to the neckline of her blouse and he was momentarily distracted.

Until she snatched them away and shoved them on her face. 'And for your information, I'm not doing this because you sucked me into it. I'm doing it for *me*. Banishing ghosts, seizing the day and all that.' She scrubbed both hands over her cheeks. 'Just so you know.'

'You'll thank me later.'

'Oh, I think it'll be you thanking me.'

She drew the words out slowly, deliberately. And if he

wasn't mistaken, provocatively, albeit a tenuous attempt. His mind immediately skipped ahead to the afternoon siesta they'd taken to enjoying over the past few days...

'I look forward to it.'

'You didn't pass out,' Damon told Kate with a glance at her as they headed back to the hotel.

'I was in your lap and facing away from you—you wouldn't know if I did.'

Wouldn't know how she felt draped over him, muscles relaxed, every part of her body in contact with his? She'd been unyielding steel the whole way down. 'I'd know.'

'Since I barely know if I did or not myself, I don't see how that's possible.'

'But you did it, Kate.'

'I did.' She leaned back against the headrest and closed her eyes.

Damon took the hint and tuned into his own thoughts. She'd never mentioned a brother. It went some way to understanding why her dad was so protective; he'd lost a son. His only son. The grief was real and lasting. Unlike his own parents who didn't give a damn. Damon wondered how it would feel to have someone to care about him. Who cared enough to cry if he didn't come home. Then he remembered something Kate had said up on the mountain. Something about not watching someone else she...what? Cared about? Or had he heard the beginning of a word that meant a lot more?

His stomach bottomed out the way it did when he launched himself into space and his breath caught in his throat. Hell, they both understood the rules. But he didn't want their physical relationship to end yet. He didn't want to go back to being her big bad boss. And her temporary boss at that. He wanted...

Feeling confused and confined, he wound down the window. The scents of South East Asia streamed in on a tide of humidity; a whiff of decaying rubbish, spicy vegetable curry, pungent tropical fruits.

What did he want? He rubbed at a tension knot at the back of his head that had developed out of nowhere. Impossible. He wanted Kate. The woman who turned his body feverish every time he looked at her. Even in those damn conservative work suits she wore. Or worn jersey and fluffy slippers. Or nothing at all. Specially in nothing at all.

He was hung up on a responsible family girl with a no-risk outlook on life. Katerina.

Now he knew the reason behind that. And he knew why they'd never fit as a couple long term. Even if he was looking for a woman to settle down with, *which he wasn't*, they were too different. In his leisure time he lived for the thrill of danger. She liked safe, both at work and play.

And yet she'd jumped with him even though she'd been terrified. Because he'd asked her to. That made her one special woman.

They arrived back at the hotel mid-afternoon. Damon crossed to the balcony and closed the shutters on the outside glare, leaving the room in cool shadow.

When he turned around Kate was loosening the braid in her hair, drawing it over her shoulders in a rippling waterfall of ebony. Her bottomless eyes were fixed on his.

His skin tightened; his body grew hard. It was always the same. One look and he was turned on. He took a step towards her, but she held up a hand.

'We leave tonight,' she said. 'Tomorrow morning we'll be home and back to being colleagues.'

In the brief hiatus he heard the elevated sound of their breathing over the ever-present silken murmur of the sea. And his heart—each beat marking the passage of time. Their last afternoon.

That same something he'd experienced earlier in the car stirred along his veins and rolled around in his gut. 'No rule says we can't change the rules, Kate. We don't have to remain just co-workers.'

'We do.' Her sigh was the only sound in the room. 'It can't be anything else. Not just because you're my boss and I don't date my boss, but because you and I want different things.'

*What do you want, Kate?* Damon asked her silently. She always made every effort to convince him her career came first, but for a beat out of time those eyes told him something else entirely. She wanted to settle down with a home and family of her own, the way all girls like her wanted.

He had no idea what home and family even meant. How could he give her that when he'd never experienced it himself? She was right. Better to keep things the way they were. The problem was, could he keep seeing her day after day and not touch her?

She took another breath and he noticed the tight buds of her nipples against the light fabric of her blouse. He saw her gaze flick to the front of his jeans.

'Right now it would seem we both want the same thing,' he said, and reached for the hem of his T-shirt.

'Don't.' Kicking off her shoes, she crossed the space between them, skimmed her thumbs up and down his forearms. 'You're always in charge. At work, in bed.' Her hands moved up over the cotton to rub light circles over his chest. 'It's payback time,' she murmured as she leaned forward to place her mouth where her hands had been, creating rosebuds of moist heat against his nipples. 'And I want a fantasy.'

'O-k-ay.' His let his arms fall to his sides. 'Never let it be said Damon Gillespie doesn't grant his woman her fantasies.' He knew his mistake the moment the words left his mouth.

*'His woman?'* she repeated with scathing effect. 'What century are you living in?' Chocolate eyes flicked to his as her teeth bit with intent into his T-shirt, nipping at flesh.

'Would you prefer the term mistress?' He jumped as the pain intensified and swore her teeth sharpened. 'Okay, okay, how about partners?'

'Very well…partner. I'm seizing the day.' She stopped biting and leaned into him, her fragrant hair brushing his arm like silk, her breasts plump cushions against his navel, but when he tried to pull her closer, she stepped back and slapped a hand on his chest. 'This is my fantasy, you'll do as I say. And keep your hands to yourself.'

Was this woman with attitude the diminutive Kate Fielding? He'd had women who liked to call the shots and he'd enjoyed it, but never so much as he did now. Although it was hardly innocent, there was a delightfully fresh naiveté about her seduction he'd never experienced before.

Her fingers crept underneath his T-shirt, smooth palms sliding over his flesh as she eased the jersey higher, sending ripples of heat to every extremity in his body. He wanted her mouth there, where her hands were. He wanted to feel her breath on his skin, to feel it quicken with desire as she touched him.

As if granting him his wish, she ran a moist tongue around his navel, then delved inside. He let out a suffocated breath as she laved a slow and sensuous pathway north, the damp warmth cooling as she travelled. His hands balled into fists at his sides. A flick of that tongue over one nipple and he groaned, one hand moving to his jeans zipper to ease the burgeoning pressure or to coax her into helping, he wasn't sure which. 'I—'

'Quiet.' One hand intercepted his and pushed it aside, causing his T-shirt to slip down unevenly. 'Take it off,' she ordered, stepping back to watch him with passion-dark eyes.

He did as she asked, cast it aside. She reached out and her fingers dipped beneath his waistband, snapping the top button and sliding down the zip, releasing his erection into cool and capable hands. He sucked in a breath. Very capable. He swore he felt each slender finger as she smoothed them down his length, creating a slippery friction that was going to tip him over the edge… 'Careful,' he warned on a harsh exhalation.

'I'm always careful. Some might say too careful.' She moved on, sliding her hands inside his jeans and coaxing them down his thighs. She stopped at his knees and looked up at him. 'Those boots—they're in the way.'

Damn. It was hard to bend down, untie and remove them without toppling over and looking like an idiot, but he managed. Barely. His jeans and jocks went too, and he straightened up to meet her eyes.

For a moment they stood eyes locked, then her gaze scanned him thoroughly from head to toe until a fine sheen of sweat filmed his entire body. His rock-hard, naked, *ready* body.

And she was still fully clothed.

'Lie on the bed,' she told him, remaining where she was. She waited until he complied. 'Are you a patient man?'

Tension coiled through him; every cell in his body screamed out for action. Now. 'Not at this particular moment, no.'

Something like laughter danced in her eyes. It made him feel… Hell, he felt vulnerable. He'd spent years overcoming that particular inadequacy. Kate had managed to dash his belief that he'd conquered it to smithereens. But it wasn't so much physical vulnerability—although that took current precedence in his naked state—but an emotional vulnerability.

Clenching his jaw, he refused to consider it, refused to surrender to it. 'Come here, Kate,' he commanded with what he hoped sounded like the full force of authority.

But instead of joining him on the bed, she walked to the door. 'Don't move a muscle,' she warned as she pulled it open. Her eyes still glistened with amusement. 'I'll be back.'

'What the…?'

He didn't bother finishing when the door closed behind her. He drew in a slow laboured breath, looked down at himself. Ready, willing and able—hadn't he mentioned that to her only hours ago? His breath rushed out and he swore, loudly and vehemently.

The tables had been well and truly turned. Was this what she meant by payback? Leaving him here sweltering in a lather of unfinished business?

# CHAPTER ELEVEN

DAMON clenched his jaw, focusing on the everyday sounds outside rather than his discomfort and ordering his body to *relax* while he considered the situation in the room's cool dimness. He'd give her five minutes tops.

The woman he'd brought back from the jump wasn't the same woman he'd set out with this morning. He'd witnessed that turnabout on the mountain. He wanted to ask her more about her brother. He wanted to ask her about her fiancé, the man who put those shadows in her eyes. About her family.

But what would be the point? Theirs wasn't that kind of relationship. One where confidences were shared along with hopes and dreams and fears. Better—*safer*—to stick to what they had. Which was? The question had him closing his eyes in frustration…

He'd meant to get up—it was obvious she'd played him—and was dozing when he heard a soft tinkle at the foot of the bed. He opened his eyes. His barely diminished erection sprang up and took notice. He had to swallow over a suddenly dry throat before he said, 'Where did you get that?'

Kate hadn't expected to find him where she'd left him and clearly he seemed as surprised about that fact as she—she'd taken longer than she'd expected. 'You can get just about anything you want in this hotel,' she said. 'Even dress-ups.'

She flicked the tiny brass discs on her bra and set them jingling. 'They have a pirate costume if you want to play too.' She eyed him all over. 'Or perhaps you'd prefer a Tarzan loin-cloth.'

He pushed up on the pillows. 'I'm happy to watch.'

She walked to the room's CD player and slid in a disc. Sultry Eastern music flowed out of the speakers. It wasn't quite the same as the music her belly-dance class used, but it sufficed.

She held Damon's gaze as she sucked in her stomach and began to slowly gyrate her hips to the fluid sound. Then faster as the tempo increased.

His eyes told her he more than liked what he saw. He was right; freedom sang sweet in her veins. Today she'd achieved something she'd never thought she could do. Perhaps she was ready to take a few more risks in her life. The question was, did those risks and that life include Damon? She swept all thought aside—now wasn't the time.

'Enough. Come here.' Damon signalled an end to the foreplay with an impatient wave.

'But I haven't even started my striptease yet.'

'I've taken all the teasing I can handle. Here.' He patted the sheet beside him. 'Right now.'

'Very well.' She shook out her hair the sexy way she'd seen girls do it in movies. 'But only on my terms.' His obvious arousal was its own reward and she was happy to oblige his impatience, but she wasn't finished playing the boss yet. She'd thought about this all the way back to the hotel. She wanted to be in control for once. All her life she'd done what other people told her, tried to please her fiancé, her family, Bryce. This was her chance.

Climbing onto the bed, she parted the filmy layers of her skirt—just a tantalising glimpse to show she was pantie-less—and straddled his thighs. And felt the hard muscles jerk beneath her legs.

She unclasped the tiny coin-embossed bra, drew it off and

let it fall on the mattress, freeing her breasts to Damon's gaze. And that was all she was allowing him. 'No hands,' she reminded him.

'Condoms…'

'No condoms. I want to feel you inside me, just you. It's okay, I'm on the Pill,' she reassured him as his eyes widened. 'You should know a sensible girl like me would take her own precautions.'

He nodded, relaxed back and lay beneath her, waiting for her next move. Control was its own aphrodisiac, she discovered as she leaned forward and lowered her top half so her nipples teased his flesh. Up and down, back and forth until they tingled with almost unbearable delight. She bit her lip to keep from making any sound that might signal her imminent capitulation.

Setting her palms on his thick, wiry wrists, she bent her head to sample him once more with mouth and tongue. She kissed her way across his chest, tasting damp and salt and man, feeling the thunderous beat of his heart against her lips and enjoying the way his chest hair tickled her nose.

'For God's sake, Kate… You're killing me here.'

Still straddling his thighs, she looked down on him.

His eyes seemed to swallow her up and suddenly it wasn't about feeling powerful and desirable any more. It wasn't about being in control any more. This was something soul deep.

He blew out a breath, disturbing the tips of her hair. 'You turn me inside out.'

'You mean Shakira turns you on.'

He shook his head slowly against the mound of pillows. 'As Shakira, but so much more as Kate.'

As Kate? Plain and boring Kate? 'You can't mean that.'

'You bet I do.' His hands reached for her skirt and searched for the fastening. 'Come on, honey, enough of the fantasy. How does this thing come off?' He found the catch and snapped it open, drawing the flimsy garment away, leaving her exposed to his gaze. 'Kate's the one I want to make love with. And I want to be able to touch her. All over.'

'And what if I'm not done with my fantasy?'

He reached for her breasts, rasping his thumbs gently over her nipples with deliberate intent. 'You're done.'

Pointless to argue. Arguing wasted time and she was as needy as he. She lowered herself slowly onto him, felt him totally naked for the first time. Felt his heat and strength fill her as she slid down his rock-hard length.

All the way to her womb. She watched his eyes watching hers, quiet, calm, and felt the connection. And took him deeper inside her, to her heart.

It only lasted a moment, that shared accord, but she knew it was dangerous. A man like Damon didn't want her heart. Didn't want anything beyond what they had. Her recklessness had got her into this situation in the first place, yet she twisted her hands into her mass of hair, lifted her buttocks and sank onto him again. And again. Over and over until she saw the calm, clear topaz in his eyes turn stormy.

Until smooth seas grew turbulent, sucking her under, then tossing her into a whirlpool that knew no sense, no reason. Only passion that swept them both into uncharted waters, because as she surrendered to the maelstrom she knew, with absolute certainty, that, willing or not, he was right there with her.

Kate watched the Opera House glistening like pink sails on Sydney Harbour as their aircraft made its final approach in the early morning sunlight. The familiar harbour ferries left white trails on the brightening water, Friday morning traffic snarls already blocking the main arterial roads and it was only seven a.m.

The last day of the working week. On Monday she'd be one of those workers. A worker whose focus was anywhere but work. Struggling with holiday enquiries metres away from the man who'd been her lover for the past ten days. Smelling his clothes, his skin if he came within coo-ee of her. Hearing his familiar deep voice in the next room—or, worse, as he leaned over her computer to talk with her, those perceptive eyes probing hers for answers she wasn't going to give.

She reached for her suit jacket and slipped her shoes on as they taxied toward the terminal. Her business attire went some way towards accomplishing her professional persona, at least outwardly.

Except she'd not been able to resist the designer shoes she'd seen at Bali International. Black, shiny and five inches high. And the way her foot arched in them made her feel oh-so-feminine.

She'd never worn such elegantly high heels before. She'd never felt so desirable before. Especially when she'd seen Damon's instant reaction.

'They're hardly practical for travel,' he pointed out at the airport even as his appreciative gaze lingered on her legs. 'You'll end up barefoot and I'll have to carry you through Sydney airport.'

'Is it worth it, though?' she tossed back.

He grinned. 'Hell, yeah.'

But it had been a big mistake wearing them on the plane. And she'd done the unthinkable—she'd dumped her sensible, comfortable work shoes in the ladies' room bin there.

Her whole adult life had revolved around support shoes. Her hip problem was also the reason behind her regular belly-dance classes. They helped keep her flexible despite Damon's accusations to the contrary on that first morning in Bali. She almost smiled at the memory. Just once she wanted to look sexy.

For herself or for Damon?

She mentally shook her head. She wasn't going to think about the way he'd looked at her. It was over.

'Do you want to stop for breakfast before you go home?' Damon's voice intruded on her thoughts. He sounded upbeat—did he think she'd change her mind about their relationship? Or was it a case of his supreme confidence in changing it for her?

She kept her gaze pinned on the Qantas jumbo taxiing the other way, rather than look at him. But she knew what she'd see—that sexy stubble she'd taken to enjoying against her skin every morning when he'd knocked on her door promptly at seven, anticipation in his eyes. 'I couldn't eat a thing.' *It'd only remind me of our shared breakfasts in bed.* 'I need to unpack and do some laundry.'

'And catch up with your family at some stage, I guess?'

'Actually I'm…flying up to Coffs Harbour tomorrow morning.' She heard the crisp coolness in her voice. 'My parents and Rosa have gone to celebrate my great aunt and uncle's golden wedding anniversary. I'm expected to put in an appearance over the weekend.'

The expectation on her parents' part—for this function at least, since they thought she was still out of the country—was an out and out lie, but it would give her time to think. Alone. The timing couldn't have been better if she really wanted space from Damon.

'You play the role of dutiful child to the hilt, don't you?' His comment held definite undertones.

'Are you criticising me because you're not guilty of the same?' She regretted the barb as soon as the words left her mouth. 'I'm sorry.' She turned to look at him, filled with remorse. How could she, when his own parents didn't acknowledge him? When his family life was non-existent? 'I shouldn't have said that.'

But the stinging words had hit their target. His mouth firmed and the furrow between his brows deepened and his eyes…she didn't want to look at his eyes…

'Why not?' he said, his voice oddly devoid of emotion. 'It's no more than the truth.'

The aircraft came to a stop and a flurry of activity ensued

as passengers gathered belongings, bodies pressed together in their haste to disembark.

Damon exited first, and she followed him off the aircraft and into the arrivals lounge cursing herself all the way. Since they'd travelled business class their luggage was already on the carousel when they arrived. They collected their gear and then headed for the escalator.

As she stepped on behind him Damon turned to her. Two steps behind, as the escalator descended, she was the same height as him. Even though it was a two-person step, she chose to remain where she was. He leaned closer; his eyes bored into hers. 'You obviously want to be on your own. Perhaps it's better if we take separate cabs.'

This was it, then. The end of their holiday ruined by her cutting remark. Suddenly the bump and grind of surrounding passengers, the smell of people cooped up all night in an aircraft made it hard to breathe. 'My apartment's on the way to Bryce's. It makes sense to travel together.'

'I'm not going back to Bryce's apartment.' His chin lifted fractionally. 'There's someplace else I need to be.' She saw something she'd never seen in his gaze before as he turned away from her.

Some*one* else, she amended silently, her hand tightening around the handle of her suitcase. She shuffled her feet impatiently. Could this damn escalator go any slower?

Then everything seemed to happen in slow motion. She felt the heel of her shoe catch in the grooves, a sharp wrench of pain in her foot…and then she was cartwheeling past Damon and unforgiving steel was rising up to meet her.

Damon rubbed a hand over his bristled jaw as he kept watch over Kate. The ambulance had brought her to the hospital and she'd been admitted for observation. Staff had informed him she had a slight concussion and a sprained ankle, but otherwise she was fine.

Right now she was sleeping it off. He couldn't see the bump on her head beneath all that hair but he was sure it was a beauty.

He was no stranger to fear, but when he'd seen Kate crumpled and unconscious at the foot of the escalator... *Not again. Never again.* He clamped his teeth together and refused to think about what might have been. *She's going to live, get over it and move on.*

But for once his will power failed him. He'd known what it was to love someone before but it hadn't been like this. Bonita hadn't made his blood pound through his veins like a kettle-drum parade. He couldn't remember whether the skin beneath Bonita's breasts had tasted sweet or even if she'd made those little noises the way Kate did when she made love.

And he'd never wanted those things with Bonita the way he wanted them with Kate. Theirs had been a tender growing-up together, resulting in the inevitable. Yet he'd loved Bonita.

Was that what he felt for Kate? Love?

The thought rolled through him like a thunderstorm, all light and noise, and every hair on his body rose. He didn't want it; he didn't know what to do with it.

He didn't know *how.*

Pushing up out of the hard visitor's chair, he paced the length of the ward and back, his boots sounding too loud, too brittle—the way his heart felt right now. He wasn't the man for her. He couldn't be that man for her. As she'd said on their last night in Bali, they wanted different things. The sooner he got Bry's business up and running again and wrapped things up, the sooner he could get back to what he did best. On his own.

He walked to the fifth-floor window and looked out over the harbour and its busy water traffic. Then down to the busy street directly below. That familiar rush skittled down his spine. He needed a diversion, something to take his mind off her. He needed a jump. And soon. As soon as Kate was better.

His neck prickled and he turned to find Kate watching him. He didn't want to analyse that look in her eyes, nor did he want to think about his own reaction to seeing it. 'You're awake.' He crossed the room and hesitated before he took her hand. It felt small and fragile in his. 'How do you feel?'

'Like I've been run over by a truck.'

'I'm not surprised.'

'My beautiful shoes.'

He had to grin. 'You have a concussion and what could have been a broken ankle or a whole lot more and you're worried about shoes?'

'I never had shoes like them before.'

'The left shoe's a write-off.' He squeezed her fingers. 'We'll buy you another pair.'

She shook her head, looking defeated. 'What time is it?' She winced as she tried to sit up.

'Take it easy.' He adjusted the pillow behind her. 'It's after three.'

A small frown creased her brows. 'You've been here since this morning?'

And still wearing the clothes he'd travelled all night in. No shower, no shave. Even with the nursing staff on hand, he wasn't leaving her bedside. 'Where else would I be?' He released her hand, suddenly awkward with the intimacy. Which made no sense considering the intimacy they'd shared over the past ten days.

Her frown deepened. 'Didn't you have to be somewhere?'

'It doesn't matter. What about your parents—you want me to ring them and say you won't be able to make it?'

'No. I don't want them to worry; they've been looking forward to this celebratory trip. I'll phone tomorrow.' A long-drawn-out sigh. 'I lied about going to Coffs Harbour.' She looked down at her hands. 'I'm sorry…about what happened at the airport.'

He looked at her for a long moment without speaking. Why

had she lied? Because she genuinely didn't want to be with him, or because she was afraid to? 'It's forgotten,' he said, finally.

He looked up as an attractive doctor appeared at the bottom of the bed, generous cleavage above a tight-fitting top and short skirt visible beneath her white coat.

The smile she gave him bordered on lethal as she flicked back her hair with a ringless left hand. 'Good afternoon. I'm Rosemary Andrews, the doctor on duty.'

He smiled back. 'How's it going, Rosemary? Damon Gillespie.'

Her gaze lingered a second longer than necessary before she turned her attention to the bed. 'How are you feeling, Kate?' Her dainty gold bracelet glinted as she shone her little light in Kate's eyes.

'My ankle hurts when I move it.'

'What about the bump on your head?'

'A bit painful.'

'Any blurred vision? Headache, nausea?'

'No.'

She clicked off the light. 'If you have someone at home to keep an eye on you I can let you go.'

'I live alone.'

'Oh.' The doc's eyes flicked towards Damon. 'In that case we'll keep—'

'I'll be looking after her.' Damon looked at Rosemary's heavily mascaraed blue eyes rather than Kate's—he wasn't sure his about-to-be patient would go along with his suggestion.

Rosemary blinked and seemed to take a moment before she said, 'She needs someone who can monitor her for the next day or so.'

'No problem.'

'In that case, I'll arrange for the paperwork.'

'Thank you.'

'You're welcome.'

Kate followed the doc's retreat with a slight frown. 'Damon, I don't th—'

'No arguments.' He cut her off with the most valid of reasons. 'Your family's away. And you need to rest. Quietly, with no distractions.'

'No distractions?' Her voice rose on an incredulous note.

'Shh.' He put a finger on her mouth to forestall any further protest. 'You want Rosemary to hear?' He shook his head when she narrowed her eyes. 'Didn't think so. I said no arguments. And no distractions—I promise.'

Kate hadn't meant to fall asleep. They'd travelled by taxi to pick up Damon's car at Bryce's apartment. Ignoring her protests, he'd bypassed the way to her apartment and kept driving. Now as her eyelids fluttered open all she saw were tall scrubby eucalypt stands, trunks pink as the sun lowered behind them. 'Where are we?'

'About an hour north of Sydney, near the Hawkesbury River.'

She turned her head and stared at the magnificent house amongst the trees. The structure sat on the edge of a steep rise. Timber and crystal building blocks, windows winking in the late sun. Some might call it austere, yet the wood gleamed like warm honey and blended beautifully with its surroundings.

She stared at it as Damon negotiated a steep driveway and stopped near a short path.

'What is this place?'

'Home for the next couple of days. How do you feel?'

'Okay.' When the throbbing in her ankle and the vague headache she wasn't admitting to went away she'd be fine.

'Yeah, right.' He didn't believe her either. 'Wait there.'

Damon climbed out of the car, rounded the bonnet and opened the door. The clean crisp scent of the Australian bush and a wood fire burning somewhere filled her nostrils. He didn't give her time to alight, picking her up and carrying her the short distance to the front door, which opened before he knocked.

A round little woman with a cloud of grey hair and lively blue eyes appeared on the doorstep. Behind her Kate could see a tall stooped guy. An old man's cardigan hung on his bony frame.

'Hi, Jenny,' Damon said with easy familiarity, then nodded at the man behind her. 'Leigh.'

A smiling Jenny turned her attention to Kate. 'And you must be Kate.'

'Kate, meet Leigh and Jenny Charlesworth. Friends of mine.'

Kate smiled back, wishing Damon would put her down and stop treating her like an invalid. 'Nice to meet you. I didn't mean to impose. Damon—'

'Impose?' Jenny's eyes widened. She started to speak, but trailed off at Damon's frown.

Kate's confusion deepened. She wanted to speak with Damon alone, to ask him why they were here, indeed imposing on his friends' hospitality, but he didn't give her a chance. He stepped inside as if he owned the place, chatting to Jenny, who followed them across the room.

Kate got a glimpse of a fire burning in an open copper-domed fireplace in the middle of the room, honey-toned wood, snatches of cream and red before she was being carried along a passageway.

Damon stopped at the first room, a few quick steps from the living area. He'd phoned ahead and, thanks to Jenny, the curtains were closed, a bedside lamp already switched on and the snowy white quilt turned down.

He set Kate on the bed, carefully removed the pair of soft shoes he'd managed to find in her bag while he'd waited at the hospital. 'Climb into bed and I'll bring your bags in later. Or would you like to get undressed first?' She stared at him, eyes wary. 'It's okay, Kate, I didn't mean—'

'Why have you brought me here?' she whispered. 'I don't know these people.'

'But I do.' He lifted her legs onto the bed, pulled the quilt over her. 'We'll talk about it later; right now you need to rest. I'll be checking on you through the night. Doctor's orders.'

'But—'

He tapped a firm finger to her lips. 'Later.' Then he pressed her tense shoulders back into the mattress, dimmed the light to its lowest setting. Because he didn't intend getting involved in explanations he knew she'd be wanting, he kissed her forehead and forced himself to walk away from her.

Jenny and Leigh were in the kitchen; he followed the sound of their voices and the fragrance of Jenny's home-baked bread. She was sliding it out of the oven as he entered.

'Is she settled, then?' She pulled off her oven mitts and skirted the table for another hug.

'I don't know about settled, but she's in bed where I can listen out and keep an eye on her.'

'I think it's both eyes you're keeping on her,' Jenny said, leaning back from his embrace to study him a little too intensely for his comfort.

'Don't want my employees suing me,' he said, winking at Leigh to avoid her gaze and reaching out to pinch off a corner of the hot bread.

Jenny slapped his hand away. 'Wait for dinner. I made a good thick stew to eat it with. When you dropped by that day two weeks ago you didn't mention anything about a girl in your life. After tea you and I are going to have a chat.'

'I'd do as she says, son,' Leigh told him.

'The way you do?' she scoffed, glaring at her husband. But Damon could see the love in their eyes as they looked at one another as clear as his own hand.

What kept these two people together for twenty or more years than he'd been alive? Damon wondered. They were complete opposites in every way. Always had been, ever since he'd been a skinny-assed kid growing up in the same street. Jenny had been his grandmother's neighbour, and, with no kids of her own, she'd taken an interest in the two boys, particularly Damon.

So he'd sit down with her—with them both—as she'd requested. A quiet nervousness gnawed through his gut at the prospect. Jenny was one very perceptive lady and he was mortally afraid she'd see something that he'd only begun to discover himself. Something he didn't want to examine, let alone lay out in the open for others to see.

# CHAPTER TWELVE

KATE drifted on the edge of sleep, warm and cosy with an 'everything's all right with the world' feeling, something she hadn't felt in a very long time. Snuggling deeper into her quilt cocoon, she shifted towards the source of that heat.

And felt the resistance of a warm and solid someone tucked up beside her. She opened her eyes. Damon. On top of her quilt and fast asleep with a mohair rug wrapped around his fully clothed form. In the early morning light, she could see his dark lashes against his cheeks, his hair was mussed, his jaw stubbled. But the crease in his brow told her he wasn't comfortable.

A quiver of sensation rippled the entire length of her body. Against all the rules, he'd slept the night with her. Yet she didn't feel the vulnerability she'd expected. She felt safe, protected. Cared for. All the worries that had plagued her about this kind of intimacy melted away. Damon was here, beside her, and everything was okay.

Damon. How could she have fallen so hard, so quickly, without a thought for the consequences? The man who was all wrong for her. The man who didn't stay in one place, who didn't want what she wanted. She hardly knew him.

But she loved his enthusiasm for life and living, the fact that he took whatever action he considered morally right and to hell with other people's opinions. He'd made her look at herself differently, forced her out of her comfort zone and taught her life wasn't all about work.

Oh, God. Everything was *not* okay—she was in big trouble. Damon stirred and a pair of golden eyes slid open. Those huge dark pupils seemed to swallow her up. Yeah, she groaned inwardly, very big trouble.

He propped a hand beneath his cheek. 'Good morning.'

'Good morning.' She swallowed the lump in her throat. It was as if he'd read her thoughts. To her dismay, tears welled in her eyes. She'd forgotten she'd told him the physical side of their relationship was over.

Instant concern puckered his brow and his free hand reached out to wipe away the bead of moisture. 'Hey, you okay? Are you hurting anywhere?'

*Only in my heart.* Kate forced a smile and ordered herself to play it light. 'No. But I'd feel better if you got naked and under the quilt with me.'

'Are you sure? You said—'

'I know what I said. Just get in.'

'Whatever you want, honey.' His voice, scratchy with sleepy desire, the feel of his fingers on her face prompted a surge of moisture between her thighs. And, oh, that sexy smile…

She slipped a hand beneath the mohair rug and under the soft fabric of his T-shirt and explored warm, smooth skin. She discovered he was wearing tracksuit pants. Simple to slide her hand under the elastic waistband…where she found him hot and hard.

She shifted against him, frustrated with the barriers of clothing and bedding, only wincing a little at the tweak in her ankle.

'Ah, Kate.' He drew back the rug, pushing down his pants and lifting the side of the quilt in an amazing display of agility for someone barely awake, and rolled in beside her.

Kate had woken and changed into a thigh-length T-shirt at some point during the night before Damon had come in, making it easy to welcome him against her. To feel his stubbled jaw as he nudged the T-shirt up with his chin. To feel its rasp against her breast while he tugged at a nipple, drawing it out with his teeth.

Lightning heat flashed to her core. She let out a helpless moan as his erection rubbed against her pelvis, another as it slid inside her like a hot knife into butter.

Where he belonged.

The rightness, each sweet intimacy a connection. Every breath she took filling her lungs with the smell of his skin, the scent of their lovemaking. He moved slowly, gently, aware of her wounds, until tenderness turned urgent, the passion crested and they rode the wave together.

'I could stay here like this all day,' she murmured, tucking her head beneath his chin when they finally lay back together again.

'Hmm.' He ran a finger over her cheek. 'You can stay here as long as you like, but I have to go in to work.'

She frowned. 'It's Saturday.'

'We've been away a while, I want to check on things, see how they've been managing without us.'

The sound of footsteps outside the door reminded Kate they weren't alone. 'You haven't told me who Jenny and Leigh are and why we're here.'

'They were Gran's neighbours. And we're here because I don't want you to be alone today.' Hauling himself out of bed, he grabbed his track pants, stepped into them. 'I'm going to take a shower.'

Kate hadn't realised she'd been dozing until Damon nibbled her neck, smelling of fresh soap, coffee and tooth-paste some time later. 'I'll see you at dinner.'

'You're leaving now?' Obviously he'd already had break-fast. She sat up, swung her legs over the side of the bed. She could hardly stay in bed all day in someone else's house. 'I want to get up.'

'Okay, here you go.' He reached for the terry robe on the end of the bed that Kate had seen in his luggage, wrapped it around her. 'There's a comfortable room you can relax in. Plenty there to keep you occupied while I'm gone.' He swung her up into his arms. 'No unnecessary walking.'

As he carried her towards the tempting aroma of coffee and kitchen sounds she looked about her. The house made the most of the surrounding view. Huge expanses of glass brought the outdoors inside. Kate admired the wood and stone work, the Native American rugs covering the walls and floor.

They found Jenny in the kitchen—a stainless steel and black masterpiece that looked like something out of a *House and Garden* magazine.

Already dressed for the day in trousers and a dark jumper, she was buttering toast. 'Ah, good morning, Kate.' She pulled out a chair for Damon to set Kate down. 'Coffee? Or would you prefer tea?'

Kate glanced at Damon, caught the twinkle in his eye. 'Coffee's fine, thank you.'

'I'm off, then,' Damon said, kissing Kate's cheek.

She wanted to fling her arms around his neck, pull him closer for one more moment. But needy wasn't what he wanted from her. Not now, not ever. Nor was it what she wanted from herself. So she blew him an air kiss. 'See you later.'

'I don't want you waiting on me, Jenny,' Kate said as Damon's footsteps faded down the passage. 'We're imposing enough on your hospitality as it is.'

'Ah, well, now, there's a story there,' she said slowly. 'I'll just get your breakfast...' She bustled to the oven, then back to the table with a breakfast that almost obliterated the plate. 'Tuck into that,' she said and sat down opposite her.

'Whoa.' Kate eyed the plate dubiously. She wasn't used to such bountifulness first thing in the morning. 'I hope I can do it justice.'

'Sure you can.'

'You have a beautiful home, here,' Kate said a few moments later as she spooned up egg. One kitchen wall was composed entirely of folding glass doors, which could be opened and led to a narrow rectangular garden pool. A wooden walkway over the water linked the kitchen with another room—an outdoor entertainment area or cosy sunroom in winter.

Jenny shook her head. 'That's where you're wrong, dear. This home isn't ours; it belongs to Damon.'

Kate's knife skidded across the china. 'Damon's?'

'He didn't tell you.' She shook her head again.

'No. He didn't. So…' Kate asked slowly, unsure how to proceed.

'Why are we living here?' Jenny folded her arms on the chrome and smoky glass-topped table, her summertime eyes soft as she looked at Kate. 'Damon bought the house eight years ago—as an investment, he said—but I know he hadn't intended investing his money in a home; he was at a very bad point in his life. Leigh had just lost his job and we were about to be evicted from our house. He put us here as caretakers. Wouldn't take one cent in rent; said it was enough that he had people he could trust looking after it while he was overseas.

'But don't worry, we won't get in your way, we live downstairs. I only come up here once a week to dust and make sure everything's okay.'

'I'm not staying,' Kate clarified quickly. 'I have my own place.'

And Damon had his, apparently. The shock still rocked her. Why hadn't she and Damon ever shared details about their past? Because they'd agreed not to. The Now was all they had, all they wanted.

Only Kate wanted more. 'When was the last time he was here?'

'Three years ago. He was only here a couple of weeks, then

he was off again.' Jenny sighed. 'It's time he stopped running, came home, put some roots down.'

Running? 'Damon's always full-on. He's not the type to back away. From anything.' Behind Jenny's blue eyes Kate saw secrets only Damon could tell her.

So Kate didn't ask. Instead, they stuck to neutral topics and when she'd finished all she could eat of her bacon and eggs and helped clean up, she hobbled behind Jenny and let her show her around Damon's home. 'He spent a fortune on all this furniture,' Jenny said, encompassing the airy living area with a sweep of her hand. 'Hired a decorator and all, yet he's never been here to enjoy it.'

There was nothing of Damon in the rooms Jenny showed her. No photos, no memorabilia. No travel souvenirs. Despite its beauty, the house seemed empty. They passed a room filled with boxes that Jenny said Damon had left when he'd bought the house and had never opened, along with some of his grandmother's disused furniture. Finally Jenny left Kate to shower and dress.

Jenny had shown Kate to the sunroom off the kitchen, with its big-screen TV, panoramic views and comfortable lounge suite where Damon expected her to spend the day, but a token twenty minutes of mindless morning TV was more than enough. She discovered a DVD/video player but no DVDs. Outdated crime books and adventure novels. She didn't want to disturb Jenny, who'd kindly offered to make lunch, but that was more than three hours away. Unable to settle, she half walked, half limped back into the house.

She stopped at what looked like Damon's bedroom, which Jenny had skipped on her tour. Its navy and taupe quilt, typically masculine, lay undisturbed on the bed. A gentle push on the partially open door revealed a chest of drawers—and the first personal items she'd seen. She stepped inside for a better look.

Two photos. One she recognised as him and Bryce as kids.

In the other he was standing beside a black-haired girl with large dark eyes, not unlike Kate herself at that age. In the photo they must have been in their mid-teens. Damon was tall and skinny, his hair longer, maybe lighter.

Beside the bed was a stack of outdated magazines. She picked up a couple. Skydiving. She shuddered and put them back. She didn't want to think about him jumping out of a plane, but lots of people did it, it was no big deal. She'd just rather not know about it.

She looked at the photo again. Who was she? She must have been important because, aside from Bryce, she was the only person he'd thought enough of to display.

'That's Bonita.'

Kate jumped guiltily at the sound of Jenny's voice. She turned and saw her in the doorway holding a bundle of what looked like letters. 'I'm afraid you've caught me out,' she said with a shaky laugh.

'I'm not spying on you, Kate. I told Damon I'd check you were okay, so I'm checking.'

'Thank you. I'm fine.' Kate turned back to the photo. 'Who is she?'

'They were school mates and best friends. I think it was more, but he's never said and I've never asked. Bonita died of leukaemia several years ago.'

'That must have been hard.'

'It changed him.'

How? Why? Had they been in love? Was that why he didn't get involved now? 'He projects this irresponsible, no-strings, fun-guy image but…I can't figure him out.'

Jenny nodded. 'Come back to the sunroom. I want to show you something.'

When they were seated, Jenny laid the bundle of papers on the couch between them. 'At Christmas Damon always sends us a card and news on what he's been up to.' She passed Kate a photo of a seedy-looking nightclub. 'He bought this run-down establishment with his share of the money he inherited when his grandmother died. This is what it looks like now.' She passed her another photo.

'I know this place,' Kate said. 'Wasn't it renovated several years ago? It's one of the most popular venues in King's Cross. Damon did this?'

'Yes. When Bonita died he sold it at a huge profit and went overseas.' Jenny passed a couple more before and after shots. Another nightclub, a row of shops. 'Each business was failing and he pulled them out of the red, got them up and running again before selling.'

Like what he was doing with Aussie Essential— Now Ultimate Journey. Kate blew out an incredulous breath. 'He never let on.'

'He has his own Internet business now. In Phoenix.' Jenny laid the final shot on Kate's lap. 'He's a very talented man.'

'I can see that. Why Phoenix? Why not here in Australia?'

'Because he's also a troubled man. All this—' she waved a hand over the photos '—is him trying to compensate for something he doesn't know he wants.' Perceptive eyes met Kate's. 'I think you might be the one to help him.'

'Me?' Her heart did a funny little flip. 'Why? What did he say?'

'It's what he didn't say.'

'No.' Kate shook her head. She was way out of his league. They were lovers, that was all. If she'd gone and fallen for him, that was her problem, not his. He didn't want anything more than casual from her. 'I can't help him.'

'But you want to. You want to understand him.'

'Yes.' Even if their relationship could never be long term, she wanted to know him better. Wanted to know the man she'd fallen for, even when he'd gone. Jenny had shown her a side of him she'd never known; perhaps she could discover more in time.

Jenny smiled. 'I think I can help.'

* * *

Damon didn't make it back till dark. As he approached his house and saw the lights twinkling from within he felt an unfamiliar sensation in his chest. A sense of homecoming. People expecting him. Jenny had phoned and told him she was holding dinner till he arrived.

Kate was there.

Kate. Was she waiting for him, as eager to see him as he was to see her? He struggled not to let the build-up of anticipation get a hold on him as he pulled into the driveway. Yes, he wanted to see her. He couldn't wait to fall into bed beside her and feel her flesh sliding against his, to taste her all over and fall asleep sated and satisfied—beneath the covers with her this time.

That was it. Had to be it, he told himself as he locked the car, headed up the little path to the front door. He'd had a scare at the hospital yesterday and overreacted. It had hurt like hell, reminding him of past times. He wouldn't allow it to happen again. That didn't mean he couldn't try and persuade Kate to let their very personal and physical relationship continue a while longer.

He opened the door and the scent of vanilla and burning eucalyptus invaded his nostrils. The living-room lights were switched off, a fire blazed in the open fireplace in the centre of the room, its copper flue reflected the dozen or so candles set strategically around the room—the source of the perfume.

And Kate. His indrawn breath stalled mid-chest. She sat on an old picnic rug in front of the fire with a long-stemmed glass of sparkling wine in each hand.

She wore something white and clingy that dipped low between her breasts—a sexy nightgown, perhaps? He hadn't been privy to what she wore when she'd slept in Bali. Bare feet peeked from beneath its hem.

He'd never seen anything more beautiful, more alluring. Her hair caught the fire's glow, its rich black reflecting gold. Her skin, as flawless as porcelain, shone. All he could hear was the crackle of smoky eucalyptus branches. And the beat of his own heart.

'Hi. Welcome home.' She patted the space beside her. 'We're having a picnic.'

'A picnic?' To his amazement, since his gut was tied up in painfully tight knots, he laughed. Still grinning, he left his laptop and briefcase by the door and crossed the room.

'Yep. Just the two of us.'

He tugged off his boots, set them aside. 'Doesn't look like any picnic I've ever been on.'

'How many picnics have you been on, Damon?' He felt his grin slip and she nodded, held out a glass. 'You're hardly an expert, then.'

'I guess not.' Keeping his eyes on hers, he took the glass, making sure his thumb grazed her fingers as he did so, then raised it. 'To homecomings and picnics.'

She followed suit. 'Homecomings and picnics.'

They sipped the obligatory first mouthful. Kate's lips glistened with the liquor as she lowered her glass. He leaned close, traced his tongue over the moisture. Sweet and tart and delicately flavoured. He was tempted to set their glasses aside and make love to her right then and there, but she'd obviously put a lot of thought into the evening. He could wait. Barely.

He pulled back. 'What's in the goodie basket?'

'Goodies. All sorts of enticing goodies.'

He lay back on one of the cushions scattered on the rug. 'Entice me.'

'O-o-kay.' She lifted the tea towel. 'We have crackers and paté, three kinds of cheese, spicy chicken wings and fresh baked bread for starters. Then there's raspberry custard trifle with grated chocolate. I think we'll start with the crackers.' She produced a knife and plastered a cracker with paté for him. 'You've never told me what business you have overseas.'

'I thought we agreed no personal history—'

'It's not history, it's current.'

True. 'I source and supply equipment for thrill sports to customers around the world.' Which gave him the time and flexibility to indulge his own interest in the sport.

She bit into her own cracker. 'Parachutes, hang-gliders, et cetera?'

'Yes. The beauty of the Internet is I don't need stock and I can work anywhere.'

'So you don't have to—' Her mobile rang nearby. She picked it up, glancing at the caller ID. 'Sorry, I have to take this.' She pressed connect. 'Hello, Dad.' Pause. 'We're back too. We're just having tea. *Yes, Damon and I.*'

For once she sounded assertive, he noted, daring her father to take issue. 'How was the party?' Another pause, then she sat up straighter. 'Oh, I…' She shook her head. 'Okay, I'll ask…' She trailed off, holding the phone tight against her chest. 'Mum and Dad want you to come to dinner on Thursday night.'

His brows rose. 'Not Tuesday?'

'They're still in Coffs Harbour.'

'Okay.' He smoothed paté onto another cracker and held it out to her.

'You don't have to,' she murmured, her eyes wide. Anxious. Not taking the cracker.

'What—are you ashamed of me?'

'Of course not.' She turned away so he couldn't read her expression and lifted the phone to her ear again. 'Dad? He'll be there. Put Mum on the line…'

It was only after she'd burbled on to them for a few moments, then disconnected, that he wondered what the hell he was letting himself in for.

*Meet The Parents.* It sounded like a movie, one he'd rather not watch. The women he'd been involved with over the past few years had never got around to inviting him home to meet the family, for which he'd been grateful. It had saved him the trouble of working up a refusal.

He thought about it again late that night while he held Kate in his arms as she slept. The picnic tea had been relaxed and enlightening. They'd finally opened up some. They'd talked about their careers; Kate had worked in the same place for years. And since she'd obviously been talking to Jenny, he elaborated on the businesses he'd owned. Then they'd talked a little about their childhood. It felt good to talk to someone after years of being a one-man band, but the mention of past lovers was carefully avoided.

But all night the upcoming dinner had been at the back of his mind. What made meeting Kate's parents different? He suspected the old man wanted to check him out, make sure he was suitable marriage material for his Katerina.

He'd be in for a disappointment. Boot him out the door if he knew what he'd done with his precious daughter within the first few moments of laying eyes on her.

Exactly what he'd do himself if he had a daughter like Katerina. If he had a daughter…like Katerina. A kid of his own. He shook away the sudden image of Kate with a tiny version of herself in her arms. But not quickly enough. It left him breathless and shaken. Where the hell had that come from?

He stared up at the ceiling and asked himself again why it was different with Kate. Simple—he wanted to meet Kate's parents because they were a part of her. To help him understand her better. To assure them he had her best interests at heart. So he'd know she'd be loved when he left.

But by Jeez… Dinner at seven. Would it be knives at eight? What was the protocol for these things nowadays?

# CHAPTER THIRTEEN

ON SUNDAY they took a leisurely drive around the surrounding Hawkesbury area in the morning and slept the afternoon away together. Damon insisted Kate take Monday off and left for work before she could think about getting ready, but in the evening he drove her back to her apartment. He'd been tempted to ask her to stay, but he knew her professional stand on the boss/employee bit. In her eyes turning up to work with him was out.

Something had changed since that first night back home when he'd slept beside her. Almost like an acceptance, an acknowledgement that what they had was more than what either of them had expected, or indeed wanted. She'd not mentioned their status in the workplace again, which left him wondering—where was their relationship headed?

He wasn't ready to give her up. But sooner or later he had to return to the US, which meant either selling the business or letting Kate manage it.

Or keeping Ultimate Journey and moving his US-based business back here. The Internet was global—all he needed was a small warehouse. He kept minimum stock. For the first time it felt like an option. Perhaps—just perhaps—he was ready to come home.

Over the next three nights he missed her when he climbed into an empty bed. He barely had time to say more than a few private words to her at work. But they shared a few intimate glances over her computer. Ate lunch together a couple of times at the coffee shop down the road. He wondered how she felt about that and whether other staff had noticed anything different.

Thursday evening arrived. It would take too long to drive the hour's journey home for a shower so he brought a clean shirt to work and changed before picking Kate up at her apartment as arranged.

He told himself there was nothing threatening about meeting a lover's parents for the first time, but tension tied knots in his stomach nevertheless as he sat in the car a moment and stared at her apartment. For starters, he'd never met a lover's parents. It implied a certain *more* to a relationship. Something ongoing. Did they have that? And was it being fair to her, knowing his lifestyle?

Still, after this evening the relationship might be history. He unfolded himself from the car and climbed the stairs to her door. The roses for her mother and the expensive bottle of aged red wine for her father lay in the boot of his car. He unbuttoned his suit jacket, buttoned it again. Tugged at his cuffs.

Hell. He'd BASE jumped off Idaho's Perrine Bridge with less stress.

His jaw tightened and the tension ratcheted up when Kate opened the door in *faded jeans and a navy T-shirt.*

'Hi,' she said slowly, eyeing him from the knot of his striped silk tie to the hem of his trousers. 'Wow.' Astonishment gave way to a smile. 'You look…good enough to eat.'

'Later,' he said, a rough edge to his voice. Why hadn't he thought to ask what to wear? 'You never wear jeans.'

Her brows rose in surprise. 'I do. You just haven't been around long enough to see.'

Okay. He could accept that. Would it be too much to ask her to go change into something that made him less of a…spectacle? he wondered. But she grabbed a fluffy jacket from the hall-stand and slammed the door shut behind her before he could get the words out.

Her smile sparkled up at him as she said, 'Let's go.'

He spun on his heel and trotted down the steps, his shiny Italian shoes beating a less-than-enthusiastic rhythm on the concrete as he headed for the passenger door. Too late to go home and change, too late to back out of this whole deal.

To keep conversation to a minimum he cranked up the volume on the car's stereo and mentally rehearsed the evening ahead. They hit heavy traffic as they travelled over the Harbour Bridge. A dull pain throbbed at the back of his head.

He saw Kate watching him from the corner of his eye. She rubbed cool fingers over the exact spot. 'You're not worried about this, are you?'

'Why would I be worried?'

He felt her shrug. 'Because this is a new or rare experience for you?'

'It's all good.' *Liar*. He tried clearing his throat, reaching up to yank off his tie, which had a stranglehold on his vocal cords.

'No.' Kate stopped him. 'You look perfect just the way you are. Don't change a thing.'

At Kate's direction, he pulled into the driveway of a modest but well-maintained home. The moment he shut off the engine, she turned and smacked her lips to his. Then leaned back and grinned at him. 'I've wanted to do that all day.'

'And you chose now? Here?' He could only wonder if her parents were watching from behind the lace curtains.

And if she'd done it deliberately, an act of defiance against the old man.

'You don't think you'll get another chance when the evening's over?'

'Oh, yeah. I do.' Her eyes lingered a moment with the promise of later. Then she was up and out.

By the time he'd retrieved the flowers and wine from the boot, she'd seen the door opening and was walking up the path. Both parents were on the veranda by the time he caught up. And wouldn't you know it? Wall-to-wall denim greeted him.

When she'd hugged them both and turned, Kate's smile faltered. 'Oh…Damon…' Her voice dropped to a whisper. 'I didn't tell you—Mum has an allergy to roses…and Dad doesn't drink.'

*Strike one.*

'Katerina!' her mother scolded. 'You're embarrassing the poor man. And how nice he looks too. I do like a man who wears a suit and tie to dinner.' She smiled, her warmth genuine. 'The flowers are a thoughtful gift. They're just beautiful—I'm so sorry I can't risk smelling them. Thank you.'

Mrs Fielding looked like an older version of Kate and younger than the fifty or more years he knew she must be. He managed a grin back. 'Guess I should've gone with the chocolates. I'll know next time.' If there *was* a next time. He set the flowers and bottle—who knew if her father was a recovering alcoholic?—on the well-scrubbed terrazzo porch. 'In that case, the roses are for you, Kate.'

'Thanks.' A moment of awkward silence.

Damon extended his hand. 'I'm Damon Gillespie—'

'Mum, Dad, this is—'

Both spoke at the same time.

'Paul and Maria,' Kate's mother said. 'Welcome, Damon, come on in, dinner's nearly ready. And Rosa sends her apologies, she won't be home till late.'

The women disappeared into the kitchen, leaving Damon with the stern-looking Paul Fielding and the aroma of tomatoes and basil wafting through the doorway. When they were seated on an uncomfortable couch in the tiny lounge room with its seventies décor, Paul said, 'So you and Katerina had a successful trip, she tells me.'

'Yes. I think we achieved a good outcome. Have you been to Bali yourself?'

'No. Never could stand long-distance flying.'

'It can be stressful,' Damon agreed. 'You've just returned from Coffs Harbour?'

'Family reunion. Shame Katerina couldn't make it. Family's important.'

'Yes.' He could feel the man sizing him up. As if he blamed Damon for Kate's lack of attendance. Paul Fielding might be a good head shorter in stature, but he more than made up for it in presence. Damon ran a finger around the inside of his collar.

'You got family, Damon?'

For a sentimental instant he wished he could count his parents as family. 'Only Bryce.'

He nodded. 'Katerina told us the news. Sorry to hear it. So you're going back to…where is it you live?'

'Phoenix, Arizona. Yes, I'll return at some point—I have business there.'

'A long way to go.' Startling blue eyes drilled into Damon's. 'I don't want my girl hurt.'

Damon felt his hackles rise. This from the man who wiped the smile from Kate's face with his phone calls, who subdued her exuberance with aggression. 'I have no intention of hurting Kate.'

'You do and you'll have me to deal with.'

The man might be overbearing, but it was plain he loved his daughter and wanted to protect her from the hurts in the world. But sometimes that wasn't possible. Everyone had to face their own demons at some point. 'I understand. But with respect, Kate's an adult, she has her own life to live.' *For Pete's sake.* And perhaps Damon should shut the hell up.

Paul snorted. 'She's soft as butter. If she can't stand up to me who will she stand up to?'

'She can hold her own in the workplace.'

'Well, good for her.' His body seemed to deflate as he let out a slow breath. 'I just want what's best for Katerina. Rosa's marrying a Frenchman; who knows how long it'll be before they decide to go back to France?' A shadow flitted across the man's expression. 'Katerina's all we have left now.'

Yes. He'd lost his only son. 'She'll be here for a long time to come, Paul. Her family's the most important thing to her.'

Paul looked at him a moment without speaking, then nodded and seemed to make an effort to lighten up. 'You a rugby, soccer or Aussie Rules man?' he asked, switching on the TV and flicking to a cable channel where a soccer game was in progress.

'I try to follow them all. Hard to get Aussie Rules in the States, though.'

They watched a few moments in almost amiable silence, caught up in the excitement of the match. The man had a hard shell, Damon decided, but inside he was as soft as Kate.

Kate had only mentioned her fiancé once, but he'd hurt that soft, vulnerable part of her. Badly. He felt a dull ache settle somewhere near his heart. *You'll hurt her too when it's time to leave Australia.* Just as her father predicted.

At ten o'clock Kate waved goodbye to her parents, breathing a sigh of relief as Damon backed sedately out of the driveway. Her mum obviously loved Damon, her dad…well, he'd take a little longer, but she sensed he respected him. As her boss of course. But as a lover?

Her thoughts came to a screeching halt as Damon pulled into the kerb less than a couple of houses down the road. Beneath the wash of the cool blue street light the glint in his eyes was positively fierce, dangerously intent. It cast the angles of jaw and cheekbones in sharp relief, but she didn't have time to question because a hand reached behind her neck, pulling her close, holding her head prisoner as he mashed his lips to hers.

She felt a desperation in his kiss she'd not felt before. A possessiveness that reached out and wound around her heart, pulling her closer. Closer.

When he at last pulled away they were both gasping for air. 'I've wanted to do that all day.' His voice was a husky echo of her earlier words. He rubbed a warm hand over the swell of her suddenly full breasts. Then both hands. Shoving the jersey up and curling his fingers over the top of her bra to find her tightly puckered nipples.

'And I want to go on doing it all night.' He lowered his mouth to her breasts. 'Let me stay with you.'

The words were an aphrodisiac, her body already humming in anticipation, but she didn't answer straight away. Her head lolled back against the headrest as his teeth teased and nibbled, as the faint pinprick of stubble rasped her skin. 'You shaved after work tonight to meet my parents.'

'Yes.' His tongue swirled around the tips, leaving moisture that cooled in the air. 'So I deserve to stay.'

'It's a single bed—too small for both of us.'

'We'll manage.' He lifted his head, straightened her clothing and sat up. Yanked his tie to one side and slipped the top button free. Then he cradled her face in his palms, raw hunger in his eyes. 'Say yes, Kate.'

She knew he wasn't for ever; he'd always been up front about that. But he'd done his best this evening to be the man he thought her parents expected him to be. Why? Had it mattered to him how they saw him, what they thought of him? As her boss, or a partner? And he'd looked so horribly uncomfortable in his suit with the roses and wine.

He'd done it for her.

'Yes,' she whispered.

She'd never had a man in this bedroom, never expected to. So she'd decorated it in pink and white and delicate furnishings. She might be thirty, but her little girl's bedroom was something she'd never had growing up. She'd shared with

Rosa and it had been utilitarian white with navy quilts, ugly gold carpet and dark second-hand furniture.

She paused at the door. 'It's a bit girly.'

'I won't be looking at the room,' he muttered, already dragging his tie off as he pressed his lips to her neck. He dropped it on the floor, and followed her through the doorway. Darkness enfolded them in its velvet embrace, intimacy surrounded them.

'Lights,' he said, his voice rough with desire. 'I want to see the woman I'm going to make love with.'

She felt her way to the bedside lamp and switched it on. A rosy light warmed the slight chill in the room, or was it Damon's own heat radiating across the space between them?

A couple of heart-thumping moments later they were naked and breast to chest, thigh to thigh on her rose-sprigged sheets. The lamp's peachy glow darkened his eyes to deep emerald and painted his tanned skin a healthy bronze.

'God, I've missed you like this,' he muttered in her ear as he slid inside her with a groan of pleasure.

Her moan of desire echoed his. 'Same here.'

His lips meshed with hers, his tongue demanding entry inside and she opened to him with a whimper. He tasted of Mum's tiramisu and dark rich coffee, strength and passion. Easy to forget that today he'd been the impatient boss with a busy schedule and no time. Tonight he was all hers.

The feel of him deep inside, stroking the very essence of her being, swept her up with him to someplace magical where angel wings brushed her limbs and molten gold flowed through her veins.

Riding the peak of passion, she looked into his eyes and her heart seemed to grow and swell until there was no room for anything else. *I love you.*

And the wonder of that knowledge as she floated gently down while he watched her, his hair mussed and silhouetted against the light, his jaw tight… He slid down beside her in the narrow bed, tucking an arm around her waist and closed his eyes.

That was it? No pillow talk? She reached out to switch off

the bedside lamp, leaving only the thin beam of a streetlight slicing between the curtains. A vague disappointment slid through her; they'd barely had time for any personal communication all week.

Was she imagining it or was he cooling off on their relationship? And yet he'd begged her to let him stay. Maybe begged was an exaggeration; she hadn't put up much resistance. He'd gone to so much effort tonight—had her father put him off? Maybe he'd decided it wasn't worth getting involved with a woman who came with conservative parents attached. Not to mention an extended family that defied counting.

He shifted slightly, but in the dimness she could see his closed eyes. The past few moments had been like a magical dream, but she forced herself to face reality. She loved him—fact number one. But loving him changed nothing—sooner or later this relationship would be over—fact number two. It was as inevitable as the sun rising tomorrow.

Damon feigned sleep but his thoughts were running at a million miles an hour. He wanted to hold her closer the way he'd grown accustomed to—was it only a few days ago? It felt like years. To rub his hands over her flesh and feel her heart beat against his palm. To press his nose into the softness of her neck and surround himself in her own special scent.

To forget what had gone before, let himself go and just love her.

But he couldn't risk it, not with his lifestyle. He'd seen that starry look in her eyes. Soft, vulnerable, fragile.

He was walking on emotional quicksand. She was getting too close, spinning dreams he couldn't give her. And if he wasn't careful they were both going down.

He had to tread carefully, take a step away. His past had already mapped out tomorrow for him. He only had now. And now was a very good time to schedule that Malaysian jump.

* * *

*Kate was falling endlessly. Sheer cliffs a fingertip away, the sound of her scream whipped away from her lips by the wind howling past her ears. Stony ground rushing up to meet her...*

She woke breathless, heart pounding, her fingers twisted in the sheets where Damon had lain. As her breath sawed in she registered the scent of soap and the very normal and comforting sound of running water.

She hadn't had that dream in a long time.

'Good morning.' Towelling his damp hair, Damon stepped into her room wearing only tiny black briefs, showcasing his rippling abdomen and muscled thighs.

'Hi.' Shaking the haunting dream images away, she glanced at her digital clock. 'You're up early. We don't have to be at work for another couple of hours.' She stretched, easing out the kinks she'd earned by being relegated to a sliver of the bed and hoping he might join her again before they had to leave.

He retrieved his shirt from the wicker chair, put it on and began doing up buttons without looking at her. 'I want to go in early, finish some work. I'm going away for the weekend.'

'Oh? You never mentioned it.' A bad feeling rolled around in the pit of her stomach. Why had he not mentioned it?

*Why should he?* They didn't have a claim on one another. But with the way it was between them, she'd have considered it a courtesy at least.

'Because it wasn't a definite until this morning,' he said, casting about for a sock.

'You arranged a trip at this hour of the morning?' She watched him shake out his trousers and step into them.

'Six a.m., actually.' His expression reminded her of the moment at the airport just before she'd fallen. She'd been cool towards him, an attempt to keep herself emotionally safe— he'd been cool right back. Had it been some sort of defence, a protective shell he surrounded himself with?

He must have interpreted her silence as condemnation

because he looked at her and said, 'I won't be taking any time off work. I'll be back first thing Monday morning.'

She reached for her flannel dressing gown at the bottom of her bed, slipped it on, tying the sash as she rose. 'Where are you going?'

'Kuala Lumpur.'

*'Malaysia?* But we just got back from Bali. Why the heck are you going there?' She had to ask.

She shouldn't have asked.

'I've organised a jump with Seb and another guy.' He found his tie, slung it around his neck. 'An event like this doesn't come up very often; it's too good an opportunity to pass up.'

That bad feeling flexed and stretched and rolled around some more. She knew he jumped. Lots of people jumped. Didn't mean she had to like it. 'We have skydiving events in Sydney, believe it or not,' she remarked caustically.

He stopped dressing and looked at her. 'It's a BASE jump.'

She was aware of a choking sound coming from her throat as she stared at him. Not a skydive but something so much more dangerous. Deadly.

'Do you know what that is?' he asked when she didn't speak. Couldn't.

An extreme sport involving jumping from fixed objects like buildings and bridges and mountains using only a single parachute. A daredevil stunt that could kill in a second. Her stomach turned to ice. 'It's suicide, that's what it is.' Her eyes drilled into his. 'I was right. You really are the thoughtless, reckless, irresponsible and *selfish* son of a bitch I thought you were.'

She thought she saw regret or remorse in his gaze. 'It'll be okay, I've done it before. Don't worry.'

'Don't worry. *Don't worry?*' Shoving her hands in her hair, she twisted away from him, couldn't bear to look at him. She pressed her lips together as the strong and bitter taste of bile rose up her throat.

She felt his hand on her shoulder. 'When you see me again it'll be at the office on Monday morning, fighting fit as usual.'

Tears clogged her voice, but she dragged in a slow, steadying breath and shook his hand off. Then she forced herself to turn and look at him. 'And if I told you I loved you and asked you not to do this, would it make a difference?'

His hand stilled on his tie, his complexion paled, accentuating the pinprick stubble that had appeared overnight. 'Oh, Kate…' Apart from the sound of her name, stunned silence filled the room. So quiet she could hear the sound of her own heart cracking.

'I am what I am.' He shook his head slowly. 'You don't want to love me.'

'You're damn right I don't, but there you are.' Her words seemed to come from somewhere outside her. 'We don't always get what we want and we don't seem to be able to choose who we fall in love with either.' She hugged her dressing gown tighter around herself and by sheer force of will she kept her eyes pinned to his.

She'd never seen Damon like this—face drawn, skin tight around his mouth. For the first time she was seeing what lay beneath the super-confident and often arrogant façade, right down to the man. But even now he was fighting against that damaged part of himself. Yes, damaged. She could see it so clearly now.

'I'm not what you need in your life, Kate.' The hunger, the raw emotion she saw in his eyes belied his words. 'You need someone who'll give you what you deserve. A home, a family.'

'I'm a career girl.' She had to believe it. Anything else, without Damon— 'Think about this while you're risking your life jumping off buildings and cliffs and heaven knows what else. There's one risk you're not willing to take, Damon. The most important, the most daring risk of all.'

# CHAPTER FOURTEEN

AFTER Damon left—without breakfast, without a word of goodbye—Kate made a decision. She was going to take the day off. Her career *wasn't* her life—too bad she'd taken so long to realise it. The irony was she had Damon to thank. She rang Sandy to tell her before Damon could arrive and take the call.

She'd never taken a day off when she wasn't physically ill. It left her feeling empty, with nothing to do and too much time on her hands. Perhaps she should have gone in. But no— seeing him would be too painful; she'd be no use to their customers at all. So she washed curtains and vacuumed floors. Scrubbed the bathroom within an inch of its life. Went to bed exhausted but unable to sleep, with the futile hope that Damon would ring and tell her he'd changed his mind.

When Saturday dawned, she knew he hadn't. So she disconnected her phones because she couldn't face talking to anyone.

Her sister let herself in later that morning and found Kate sitting at the kitchen table staring at the clock. 'I thought we were going shopping,' Rosa said, looking her over. 'Your phone's not working, your mobile's off…what's wrong?'

Kate looked at her and the tears she'd dammed up sprang free. 'Rose, I've done something stupid.'

Rosa sat down next to her and stroked her hair. 'What is it, Kate?'

'I've gone and fallen in love.'

A moment of silence. 'Oh, Katie.' Another pause. 'Would I be right in guessing it's Damon Gillespie?'

Kate nodded, grabbed a tissue from the box on the table. 'My *boss*. You know my rules about romance in the workplace—after what happened with Nick.'

'Nick was a bastard. Still is, always will be. But it doesn't have to be that way. People fall in love with guys at work all the time.'

Kate swiped at her leaky eyes. 'Not me. You'd think I'd have learnt my lesson.'

Rosa's eyes filled with sympathy. 'I take it Damon doesn't return the feeling.'

'I don't think he knows what he feels.' Lately she'd seen something in his eyes, heard something in his voice. And, oh, when he made love to her... But knowing Damon, he probably made every woman he slept with feel special. She shredded the tissue between her fingers. 'He's all wrong for me, Rose. What is it with me and my judgement of men?'

'We haven't had a chance to talk about this particular one. Why don't you tell me about him?'

Kate felt her mouth curve into a tiny sad smile at that. 'You got three hours?'

Rosa grabbed Kate's hand and began tugging her to the sofa. 'I've got all day.'

The odour of sweat and adrenaline spiked the air inside the elevator as it shot its load of BASE jumpers to the top of the KL Tower. Damon, Seb and Seb's mate Brad had strapped on single parachutes for the ride down and now mingled with others on the open-air deck. The concrete ledge where they'd launch themselves into thin air was only a few steps away.

*Kate.* Damon's heart hammered harder against his chest and he rubbed a hand over his face. *If I told you I loved you and asked you not to do this, would it make a difference?*

'Hey, Damo, what's up? You're not going soft on us now, are you?' Rolling his shoulders, Seb eyed him curiously.

Damon clenched and unclenched his hands, did a neck stretch. 'Right behind you.'

'Okay, see you guys at the bottom.' Seb grinned, then stepped up onto the ledge. Brad and Damon followed.

Damon watched Seb, high winds plucking at his shirt-sleeves. Seb hurled himself into space, then Brad several seconds later. 'Too close,' Damon swore beneath his breath. His palms, his back, itched with sweat as he watched them plummet towards the ground for five seconds…six… He let out a sigh as each guy's parachute unfurled. Those few seconds of tense waiting were the worst. Kate had had a brother she still mourned who'd died in similar circumstances and right now he understood something of how she felt.

He watched them growing smaller by the second, Brad veering close to the tower's wall, but managing to steer himself out of trouble.

He grabbed the back of his neck with his hand as voices and bodies swirled behind him. Damn it, why wasn't he jumping? Any moment they were going to ask him to step off or step aside. *Kate.* An image of her tumbling down the escalator and landing in a crumpled heap zapped through his mind. He remembered that instant of terror, the feeling of helplessness at not being able to catch her, to absorb her pain as his own.

He blinked the sweat and thoughts away, straightened, swaying slightly on the ledge. The city of Kuala Lumpur sprawled beneath him, the Petronas Towers shimmered in the heat haze in the distance. Another step as the wind whipped around his parachute pack, threatening his balance. *Jump before it's too late. Carpe Diem. Now* was what he lived for. *Now* was all that mattered. Taking risks was his life.

*There's one risk you're not willing to take. The most important, the most daring risk of all.*

Kate's wisdom.

Kate's pain.

Kate's love.

And the blazingly honest truth. It almost blinded him with its clarity, damn near knocked him sideways with its force.

He'd chosen one hell of a moment for an epiphany.

He inched back carefully. Almost too carefully. The instant he was back on the deck, he unclipped his parachute pack, handed it to an astonished jumper and hurried back to the elevator.

There *was* a future. And for the first time in years he had something worth living for.

Sydney airport teemed with passengers leaving on early morning flights as he exited. He'd showered and changed in the terminal before getting his car out of long-term parking and heading straight to work. His hopes of surprising her at home had been dashed by the aircraft's late arrival.

He had big plans for the evening. Huge plans. Starting with dinner in one of Sydney's best-known restaurants, then after he'd wined and dined her…he'd tell her what he should have told her before he left. What he'd been too afraid to admit even to himself, let alone acknowledge aloud.

He felt like a different man. He *was* a different man.

Right now he was an impatient man who couldn't wait to make up for the time he'd wasted. He straightened his tie, then glanced at his watch as he entered the office. Kate's chair was vacant, her computer screen blank. Disappointment stabbed at him. She'd missed work on Friday—his fault—but, knowing Kate's work ethic, he'd expected her here bright and early.

Sandy was in her favourite spot by the coffee machine. She smiled her million-kilowatt smile at him over her steaming cappuccino. 'Hi there, Damon.'

'Good morning, Sandy. Kate not here yet?'

She lifted her mug in the direction of the door. 'You missed her.'

Was it that obvious? 'Did she—?'

'She dropped in for a few moments, then walked out with a bag of stuff. About twenty minutes ago.'

He felt his smile fade and a niggle of doubt crept in just below his breastbone. He wasn't in the mood for puzzles. Eight hours of flying and no sleep suddenly caught up with him, dulling the morning's gloss. 'Did she say where she was going or when she'd be back?'

Sandy gave one of her neat little shoulder lifts. 'I saw her leave something on Bry—on your desk. Then she just said goodbye.'

'Okay. Thanks.' The niggle morphed and kicked and weighed like lead in his gut. He headed to his office.

'Did you sack her?'

He turned in his doorway to stare at Sandy. 'Why would you ask that?'

She sipped the froth on her coffee, watching him. 'It's just that she took Smiley with her.'

'Smiley?'

'That pink hairy sunflower thing she keeps on her desk.'

The lump rose to his throat, choking off his air. He had to swallow hard to regain what little he suddenly had left of his composure. 'No. I didn't sack her.'

A framed photograph. She'd left him a photograph of the two of them sharing a cocktail at a Balinese nightclub. He picked it up and what he saw made his chest tighten, his hands tremble. He might not have seen it at the time but there were stars in Kate's eyes. More—much more—there were stars in his. Anyone who looked could see he was in love. Entranced. Besotted. Hopelessly in love. With Kate.

What a blind idiot he'd been. He caressed her image with his thumb. 'We can still have it, Kate.'

Setting it down, he yanked off his tie, tossed it on the desk and dug out his car keys. Urgency pumped through his veins. He had to find her—

'You're Damon Gillespie?'

A woman stood at his door, barring his way. Medium height, black hair, a firestorm in her dark eyes.

He skirted the desk. Impatience snapped at his heels. 'Yes.'

'Wherever you're going, you'll hear me out first.' She stepped all the way in, closed the door. 'I'm Rosa Fielding.' She kept walking until she reached him, drilled his chest with a purple-lacquered fingernail. 'You hurt my big sister, you deal with me.'

Damon's brow rose. 'So the whole family's in on this.'

'That's what families do, Mr Gillespie. It's what we do for people we love—support them any way we can. But I *might* forgive you because Kate filled me in on your background and maybe you don't recognise love when it's right in front of you. You may not understand how it feels to—'

'Okay.' He gestured with an unsteady hand. 'Why don't you take a seat—?'

'I'd rather stand, thanks. This won't take long.'

He, on the other hand, didn't want to stand. He felt as if he'd been strung up and hung out. Hitching his butt on the edge of the desk, he ran damp palms down the front of his trousers.

'Kate's been a loyal employee here for years,' Rosa went on. 'Your uncle promised her the manager's position from this month and now she's throwing it away.'

'What do you mean?'

'She's considering another job. It might take her years to work her way up the ladder again.'

Rosa's words hit him like a hammer. Kate couldn't leave Ultimate Journey; they needed her. *He* needed her. So why was he saying, 'An agent with her skills and experience will walk straight into a good position.'

Her eyes flashed. 'You don't care if she leaves?'

'Of course I *care*.' His voice roughened as emotion battered at him. 'But if that's what Kate wants, then she should go for it. I want her to be happy.' What was left of his strength seemed to drain out of him.

'Changing jobs won't make her happy,' Rosa said more gently. She picked up the photo on his desk, studied it a moment. 'She looks happy here. So do you.' She nodded and thrust the photo at his chest. 'I'd get a move on before it's too late.'

Kate's car was missing at her apartment. Thirty minutes later he drove past her parents' house. No sign of her there either. He drummed impatient fingers on the wheel. Where was she? Which agency was she considering? He'd go back to her apartment and resign himself to waiting on her front doorstep. Except he'd never been a man who could sit around and wait.

He passed Ultimate Journey again on the off chance that she'd come back. No luck. He rubbed the tension at the back of his neck and found himself driving past the agency they'd staked out not so long ago.

A car similar to Kate's was parked nearby. He skidded to a stop, ignoring the blast from the car behind him as he scanned the area, his heart jumping into his throat when he saw a lone figure sitting on a swing in the playground. A woman in jeans and jumper with jet-black hair…

'You *are* aware you're required to give two weeks' notice before you leave, aren't you?' Kate's heart leapt at the familiar low-timbred voice as Damon sat down on the swing next to hers. Relief at seeing him whole and unharmed pumped through her, turning her limbs to liquid.

Not that she looked—it was enough he was there. *Remember what he's been doing. Reckless and irresponsible. You can't live with that.* 'I'm aware of the requirements. I'm choosing to ignore them. So sue me.' She pushed the point of her shoe into the bark chips and set herself swinging.

'I didn't jump.'

Those three words made the hair on the nape of her neck stand up. She wanted to whoop and cry at the same time. She did neither. Just kept pushing off with her foot, back and forth, as if she weren't falling apart, as if her heart weren't pounding out of her body. 'Don't tell me daredevil Damon Gillespie lost his nerve?'

'No.'

Of course he hadn't. Damon had nerves of steel. *Why then?* 'So what happened?'

'I thought of you.'

She stopped pushing. His voice had softened on the last word, making her heart beat erratically.

'What you said kept playing over and over in my head.'

She couldn't recall what she'd said because her mind was spinning and scattered like the autumn leaves at her feet. It was Damon's words that had been indelibly imprinted in her mind and the reason this turnabout wouldn't work.

'And *you* said, *"I am what I am."*' She looked at him for the first time since he'd sat down beside her. And her heart wept. 'So I hope you didn't back out on my account because if you did, it doesn't change a thing. You give up who you are, your dreams and what you want out of life, and sooner or later you'll resent it. And resent me.'

'I didn't change my mind for you, or because you asked me to. I've always made my own decisions, based on what's best for me.' He shrugged. 'Call me a selfish bastard because it's true. But that's because there was no one in my life to consider. Until now.'

*Too much.* She set the swing in motion again. Her body was jittering; she didn't know what to do with all the emotion in her chest. He reached out, brought the swing to an abrupt stop. Yanked it towards him so his face was a fingertip away, his eyes burning into hers.

'Do you understand, Kate? I changed my mind *because* of

you. I didn't get it until I stood on the edge of a concrete wall nearly a quarter of a mile up and looked down.'

A lone finger of horror stroked the back of her neck at the image. 'Get what?'

'What you said before I left. It kept niggling at me, wouldn't let me rest. Idiot that I am, I didn't realise what you meant until the last moment. That love is the most important risk you'll ever take.

'You're what I want, Kate. All I need.' He slid off his swing to crouch down in front of her, his eyes fused with hers, his breath warm against her face in the cool autumn air. 'I've lived for the adrenaline rush for so long I forgot there's more to life than hurling oneself into space. Fact is, I don't want to do it any more.'

He stroked her face, just once, a touch that arrowed straight to her heart, but she refused to let it sway her. 'I'm glad, Damon. Really I am. That I helped you in some small way.'

'*Small?*' He shook his head, covered her hand with his. 'There you go, devaluing yourself again. Tonight, Kate. Tonight we're going out for the best dinner you ever had, and then I'm going to—'

'I can't tonight, Damon.'

Damon stilled at her refusal. Stunned at the unexpected setback to his plans. 'Of course you can.'

'No. I promised my cousin Sean I'd see *Don Giovanni* with him at the Opera House.'

'Cancel.' He knew he sounded abrupt and authoritative; he didn't care.

She shook her head. 'He's already bought the tickets.'

'But you knew I'd be back tonight.'

'Yes. I did.' Unflinching eyes met his and everything inside him turned cold. His hand dropped away from hers.

'And even if he hadn't already forked out megabucks, even if we'd only planned an after-work burger I wouldn't cancel.' She rubbed her arms as if to ward off more than the autumn chill. 'You weren't willing to call off your jump when I asked you for the most valid and important of reasons. I simply wasn't a priority on your list.' She glanced at her watch. 'I have an appointment in an hour. I'd better be going.'

He stepped back. 'Not a job interview.' *Don't let it be a job interview.*

She studied him a long moment without speaking, then stood. 'Would it matter? Damon Gillespie doesn't need anyone.'

He damn well deserved that, but it didn't make it any easier to take. 'You're wrong, Kate. And I intend to prove it to you. Tomorrow night.'

'Tuesday night I—'

He jerked forward, leaned in. 'I don't care if the Prime Minister's dining with your family tomorrow night, you're making time for me.'

She blinked. 'Okay. Shall we say nine o'clock at my place?' Her voice was calm, unlike his, but he could detect the faintest tremor beneath the words.

'Eight.'

'Eight-thirty.'

'I'll be there at eight. I can wait.'

'Suit yourself. I'll see you then.' She slid off the swing, dusted off her backside.

'I take it you're not coming in to work tomorrow, then?' He swiped the back of his neck as she walked away without replying. 'Fine. That's fine,' he murmured to her retreating back. 'The rest will do you good.'

Walking away from Damon and not looking back was the hardest thing Kate had ever done. Looking back would have made it impossible. He loved her. He really did. She'd seen it in his eyes, heard it in his voice. But if it was ever going to work between them, Damon had to learn a few home truths about himself. About relationships.

So she kept her appointment for a long-overdue massage

and tried her best to enjoy the opera. Sean was a sweetheart as always, absolutely refusing to take any payment for the tickets and picking her up like a real date. And a gorgeous one at that; tall, dark and handsome with whisky eyes and a grin that would melt hearts.

She thought of another grin that melted hearts as Sean dropped her off outside her apartment and her own heart cramped with longing. 'Thanks for coming with me at such short notice. I really needed to be anywhere but at my apartment tonight.'

'Any time, Kate.' He glanced at her front door, then frowned. 'You expecting company?'

'No.' She followed his gaze to the silhouette of a man sitting on her step and her pulse accelerated. 'Yes.'

'So that's him.' His eyes narrowed. 'You want me to beat him up for you?'

'No. I think he's suffering enough.' The blow to his masculine pride was something she'd bet Damon didn't experience often. Women would not walk away from him; it would be the other way round. 'Thanks, Sean. I'll see you later.'

How long had he been sitting on her concrete step? she wondered as she approached her door. He must be freezing. She stopped as he rose. His eyes…there was a storm of emotion in his eyes. 'I thought we made it Tuesday night.' She kept her voice casual, but her heart was pounding in her ears.

'I've never been a patient man.' He held up a paper bag. 'Can I come inside?'

She nodded, stepping past him to open the door. Removing her jacket as she walked to the kitchen and sat at the table. Damon withdrew a fat candle, lit it, then turned off the light, leaving the room bathed in candlelight.

'Time to talk, Kate. We agreed we wouldn't delve into our personal history, but I think it's time, don't you?'

She did; oh, she did. But she let the silence stretch out a moment. Then she said, 'Tell me about Bonita. It was her you were thinking about that day on the cliffs at Diamond Bay, wasn't it?'

He nodded. 'Bonita and I grew up together. She was all I had. Bryce and I had little in common. We became lovers when she was only fifteen. When she died it was like a black hole had dropped into my life. It made me realise you could be dead tomorrow.'

'No one knows how long they'll live.' Her voice trembled. 'It's what we do while we're here that's important.'

'And that includes love,' he said, reaching for her white-knuckled hand clenched on her lap. 'Because without it, it's not really living. It took finding you to work that out.' Scarcely drawing breath, he went on. 'Talk to me about Nick.'

She swallowed. 'Nick and I worked at the same travel agency. We were colleagues. He was gorgeous and sexy and it was always a wonder to me that he loved someone like me. Or so I thought. Until we went on an educational. What I didn't know was that one of the colleagues travelling with us was also his bit on the side.'

He tightened his hand over hers. 'Kate…'

'Everyone at the office knew. Except me. Nobody told me, Damon. They were laughing behind my back. I didn't find out until he left me to marry his pregnant mistress.'

'So that's why you're so hung up about office romance.'

She stared at the flame, remembering the hurt, the humiliation. 'If she hadn't gotten pregnant first I would have married him, given up work and had his children. I was made a fool of.'

'No. He was the lowest form of slime. And I'm glad he left because it opened the way for me. My life would have gone on as usual until I flung myself off something one time too many. And I'd never have met you.'

Happiness blossomed inside her, but still she couldn't let herself believe. She had to say it all, bare it all.

Because she wanted it all.

'I wanted a career as well as marriage. I still want that.'

She let out a long silent breath. She'd said it. Blown any chance she'd had with him. An ongoing affair was one thing, marriage was something else—

'You *can* have both. The agency needs a manager. And I need you.' He grasped both hands in his. 'I want you and me and kids. Marry me, Kate.'

'Marry you.' Kate felt as if she were the one standing on the edge of that tower. She were the one afraid to jump. 'I work here, you live overseas.'

'I have an Internet business; I can base myself anywhere I choose. All I need is a computer. And you.' Damon reached out to stroke a fine strand of hair lying on her cheek, searching for an answer in her eyes. 'What do you say? You want to take that risk with me?'

'I…'

Damon clenched his jaw. Hell. Her trembled response wasn't the one he'd hoped for. Once he made up his mind something was going to happen, he stopped at nothing until it did and this was no exception. Especially this—it was the single most important thing that he was ever going to make happen in his life. 'Maybe this'll show you I'm serious,' he said, and dug into the paper bag.

She took it from him, then frowned. 'An *onion*?'

He loved it when her brow puckered like that; it made him want to stroke the little crease with a finger. So he indulged himself in that simple pleasure while he searched her eyes. 'A daffodil bulb.'

He loved every detail of her face from the soul-searching eyes and the little mole beneath, to the perfect mouth that plumped and softened as he said, 'I want to put down roots with you. When it flowers in spring I want us to be married. Six months, Kate, to decide.'

She caressed the bulb's papery texture, then looked up at him, eyes shining and alive. No shadows. 'I don't need six months to decide.' She leaned forward and touched her lips to his.

The sweetest kiss he'd ever known. Filled with promise and sunshine and ever afters he'd thought he'd never needed.

Finally she drew back, her eyes dancing. 'Though I might need six months to plan a wedding. A Big Fat Italian Wedding.'

'Whatever you want, *Katerina*.' He couldn't resist kissing those smiling lips again. 'Which reminds me, I guess I'll have to do the right thing and face your father.'

'He'll be thrilled. And Mum. And Rosa.'

'Ah, Rosa came by the agency today.'

Kate's lips twitched. 'I told her not to, but she never listens to her big sister.'

He smiled at that. 'She's a force to be reckoned with. I'd like her on my side in an argument.'

'Why don't we go see them now?'

'*Now?* Won't tomorrow night be soon enough?'

'You live in the Now, don't you?'

'Not just the Now any more…although Right Now's feeling pretty darn good.' He slid his arms around her, coaxing her off her chair and onto his lap, right up close to his heart. 'We have a future to plan…' he kissed her cheek, her eyes, and finally her lips '…starting with what we might do for the next hour.'

'Mmm.' She rubbed her lips against his and smiled up into his eyes. 'Or two.' She caressed his gift again. 'Tomorrow I'm going to plant this bulb. In a bright blue pot where we can watch it grow. And when it blooms I'm going to carry it down the aisle. To you.'

He rose, sweeping her up with him, and turned towards the bedroom. 'Better get started, then. The future's waiting.' And it had never looked so bright.

* * * * *

*Turn the page for an exclusive extract from*
*RAFFAELE: TAMING HIS TEMPESTUOUS VIRGIN*
*by*
*Sandra Marton*

"IN THAT CASE," Don Cordiano said, "I give my daughter's hand to my faithful second in command, Antonio Giglio."

At last, the woman's head came up. "No," she whispered. "No," she said again, and the cry grew, gained strength, until she was shrieking it. "No! No! No!"

Rafe stared at her. No wonder she'd sounded familiar. Those wide, violet eyes. The small, straight nose. The sculpted cheekbones, the lush, rosy mouth...

"Wait a minute," Rafe said, "just wait one damned minute…."

Chiara swung toward him. The American knew. Not that it mattered. She was trapped. Trapped! Giglio was an enormous blob of flesh; he had wet-looking red lips and his face was always sweaty. But it was his eyes that made her shudder, and he had taken to watching her with a boldness that was terrifying. She had to do something….

Desperate, she wrenched her hand from her father's.

"I will tell you the truth, Papa. You cannot give me to Giglio. You see—you see, the American and I have already met."

"You're damned right we have," Rafe said furiously. "On the road coming here. Your daughter stepped out of the trees and—"

"I only meant to greet him. As a gesture of—of goodwill." She swallowed hard. Her eyes met Rafe's and a long-forgotten memory swept through him: being caught in a firefight in some miserable hellhole of a country when a terrified cat, eyes wild with fear, had suddenly, inexplicably run into the middle of it. "But—but he—he took advantage."

Rafe strode toward her. "Try telling your old man what really happened!"

"What *really* happened," she said in a shaky whisper, "is that…is that right there, in his car—right there, Papa, Signor Orsini tried to seduce me!"

Giglio cursed. Don Cordiano roared. Rafe would have said, "You're crazy, all of you," but Chiara Cordiano's dark lashes fluttered and she fainted, straight into his arms.

\* \* \* \* \*

*Be sure to look for*
*RAFFAELE: TAMING HIS TEMPESTUOUS VIRGIN*
*by Sandra Marton*
*available November 2009*
*from Harlequin Presents®!*

*Darkly handsome—proud and arrogant*
*The perfect Sicilian husbands!*

# RAFFAELE: TAMING HIS TEMPESTUOUS VIRGIN

*by*

# Sandra Marton

The patriarch of a powerful Sicilian dynasty,
Cesare Orsini, has fallen ill, and he wants atonement
before he dies. One by one he sends for his sons—
he has a mission for each to help him clear his
conscience. But the tasks they undertake will
change their lives for ever!

Book #2869

Available November 2009

---

Pick up the next installment from Sandra Marton

**DANTE: CLAIMING HIS SECRET LOVE-CHILD**

December 2009

HP12869

## TWO CROWNS, TWO ISLANDS, ONE LEGACY

*A royal family torn apart by pride and its lust for power, reunited by purity and passion*

Look for the next passionate adventure in
The Royal House of Karedes:

### THE GREEK BILLIONAIRE'S INNOCENT PRINCESS
*by Chantelle Shaw, November 2009*

### THE FUTURE KING'S LOVE-CHILD
*by Melanie Milburne, December 2009*

### RUTHLESS BOSS, ROYAL MISTRESS
*by Natalie Anderson, January 2010*

### THE DESERT KING'S HOUSEKEEPER BRIDE
*by Carol Marinelli, February 2010*

# You're invited to join our Tell Harlequin Reader Panel!

By joining our new reader panel you will:

- Receive Harlequin® books—they are FREE and yours to keep with no obligation to purchase anything!
- Participate in fun online surveys
- Exchange opinions and ideas with women just like you
- Have a say in our new book ideas and help us publish the best in women's fiction

*In addition, you will have a chance to win great prizes and receive special gifts! See Web site for details. Some conditions apply. Space is limited.*

To join, visit us at

## www.TellHarlequin.com.

# REQUEST YOUR FREE BOOKS!

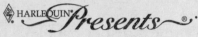

## 2 FREE NOVELS
## PLUS 2
## FREE GIFTS!

**YES!** Please send me 2 FREE Harlequin Presents® novels and my 2 FREE gifts (gifts are worth about $10). After receiving them, if I don't wish to receive any more books, I can return the shipping statement marked "cancel". If I don't cancel, I will receive 6 brand-new novels every month and be billed just $4.05 per book in the U.S. or $4.74 per book in Canada. That's a savings of close to 15% off the cover price! It's quite a bargain! Shipping and handling is just 50¢ per book*. I understand that accepting the 2 free books and gifts places me under no obligation to buy anything. I can always return a shipment and cancel at any time. Even if I never buy another book, the two free books and gifts are mine to keep forever.

106 HDN EYRQ   306 HDN EYR2

| | | |
|---|---|---|
| Name | (PLEASE PRINT) | |
| Address | | Apt. # |
| City | State/Prov. | Zip/Postal Code |

Signature (if under 18, a parent or guardian must sign)

### Mail to the **Harlequin Reader Service:**
**IN U.S.A.:** P.O. Box 1867, Buffalo, NY 14240-1867
**IN CANADA:** P.O. Box 609, Fort Erie, Ontario L2A 5X3

Not valid to current subscribers of Harlequin Presents books.

**Are you a current subscriber of Harlequin Presents books and want to receive the larger-print edition? Call 1-800-873-8635 today!**

* Terms and prices subject to change without notice. Prices do not include applicable taxes. Sales tax applicable in N.Y. Canadian residents will be charged applicable provincial taxes and GST. Offer not valid in Quebec. This offer is limited to one order per household. All orders subject to approval. Credit or debit balances in a customer's account(s) may be offset by any other outstanding balance owed by or to the customer. Please allow 4 to 6 weeks for delivery. Offer available while quantities last.

**Your Privacy:** Harlequin Books is committed to protecting your privacy. Our Privacy Policy is available online at www.eHarlequin.com or upon request from the Reader Service. From time to time we make our lists of customers available to reputable third parties who may have a product or service of interest to you. If you would prefer we not share your name and address, please check here. ☐

HP09R

I ♥ HARLEQUIN® Presents

# BROUGHT TO YOU BY FANS OF HARLEQUIN PRESENTS.

We are its editors and authors
and biggest fans—and we'd
love to hear from YOU!

## Subscribe today to our online blog at
## www.iheartpresents.com